Single Girls

EXCERPTS

~~~ I0537833

Single Handed

I made my lips curve up so they wouldn't worry about me. "Thanks. You guys should get going. Don't want you two to scare him off."

"He doesn't look scared to me." Brittany nudged me with her elbow.

I followed the path of Brittany's gaze to Tommy waving from across the lot. He pointed to his backpack over his shoulder, then to his car and I nodded.

"Even if this goes nowhere and you stay friends, at least you'll have something pretty to look at." Laynie sighed.

"Would you both stop staring?" I scowled.

Brittany nudged my shoulder. "You can't blame us. He's super cute."

"True." I wiggled my fingers, hoping to shake out the tension. "Oh, hell, here he comes."

"You'll be fine." Laynie squeezed my shoulder. "He obviously likes you exactly as you are. Just roll with it."

Brittany and Laynie waved as they strolled to their own cars. I wiped my palms on my jeans and turned to face Tommy.

Singled Out

"At least you and Wyatt are talking. That's progress," Laynie said.

Not if he didn't regret what he'd done. "I know you two meant well, but you can't force this. I'll call you tomorrow."

"Brittany, wait." Laynie grabbed my hand. "Maybe he just needs more time."

He'd had almost a year to reflect on all the ways he'd screwed up. "He's not getting more time. And you two are backing off." I longed for a hole to crawl into.

"Okay, fine," Alex said, folding her arms over her chest.

"Wait. I drove and no way am I letting you walk almost a mile in the dark." Still holding my hand, Laynie gave it a squeeze. "Hang on. I'll get my purse."

She released me and I made a beeline to the front door. I stepped outside, the crisp night air tickling my cheeks.

Alex's front door slammed just as I stepped off the porch and landed on the narrow path that divided the lawn. Assuming Laynie was right behind me, I continued walking toward her car across the street.

"Brittany!"

My breath hitched at Wyatt's voice.

Single-minded

If he really was interested, I'd put money on his reason being that I was one of the few girls who didn't try to hook up with him. That wasn't a good enough reason for me to risk getting dumped.

Or maybe he wasn't coming onto me at all... I could feel my eyebrows straining to meet in the middle as I struggled to figure out what he was up to. "Is something wrong? You're acting freaky."

"You're not getting it." He studied me. "I don't want to date other girls."

I was more confused than ever. "You're switching teams?"

"No." Josh moved closer, reached a hand out to take my glass, then he set it on the counter. Bringing both of his hands up to cup my neck, he bent toward me. "Just narrowing my focus."

My eyes bulged and I froze, incapable of stopping what I knew was about to happen.

Not that I wanted to stop it.

Single Girls

Veronica Blade

Single Girls

Crush Publishing, Inc.
Gardnerville, NV 89460
www.CrushPublishing.com

Crush Publishing, Inc name and logo are trademarks of Crush Publishing, Inc and are used only with its permission.

The places, characters and events portrayed in this book are fictitious. Any similarity to real persons, living or dead, is coincidental and not intended by author.

ISBN 978-0-9910756-1-4

Cover design by Rose Nomura
Cover Image from NovelStock.com

Printed in the United States of America

Single Girls
A Collection

Includes:
Single-handed p.1
Singled Out p.21
Single-minded p.59

By
Veronica Blade

PUBLISHING

Gardnerville, Nevada

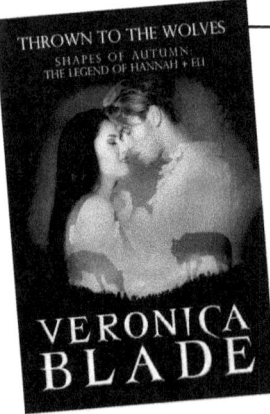

Free e-Book Offer

For a limited time, *Thrown To The Wolves: The Legend of Hannah & Eli (Shapes of Autumn Prequel)* is available for free from my website.

Find out more at VeronicaBlade.com

For Megan Durrence
I freakin' love you!!

Single Handed

Veronica Blade

Chapter One

Every day at lunch, weather permitting, Laynie, Brittany and I claimed the same table against the outside wall of the school building. The three of us shared the bench since it had the best view to watch everyone else. Today, my two best friends insisted on matchmaking for me. I'd given up on getting asked to prom, but they still had hope for me.

"You're so lucky, Alex." Laynie's gaze landed on a head of short, dark blond hair. She planted her elbows on the lunch table, rested her chin in her palms and sighed. "Tommy's dreamy."

"Lucky? He doesn't like me that way. Trust me," I said, taking a sip of my soda. "You guys are wasting your time."

"Yeah, he does." Laynie craned her neck to see past Brittany who sat between us, then turned to refocus on Tommy. "He can't resist your Latina hotness."

I choked on a gulp of my drink and coughed. "You're delusional."

"He's got this scholarly kind of deliciousness about him." Laynie said, still staring at Tommy. "Don't you think?"

Brittany flipped her blond hair over her shoulder and snuck another peek at Tommy. "Doesn't matter how cute he is, you can still kick his ass, Alex."

Yep, I probably could. That was exactly why he would never ask me to prom. Since last year, guys saw me coming and detoured. It was as if *Caution!* was stamped on a big orange sign on my forehead. I mean, geez, I saved a boy from being ganged up on by Wes Hampton and his posse. Sure, Wes had ended up face down on the concrete with his arms behind him and my knee in his back, but I hadn't hurt him. No bruises or anything.

Incidents didn't happen often, but it only needed to happen once and it spread though school faster than Mr. Fargo could write an 'F' on my calculus quiz.

My single-handed defense of weaker kids had brought our school violence down to almost nothing. The upside was how well the other kids treated me — none who I felt were prospects for prom though.

When a hundred-pound girl just over five feet neutralizes a guy nearly twice her weight, potential boyfriends tend to write the girl off. And who could blame them? Tommy was the exception, but he'd never flirted with me or hinted that he liked me as more than a friend.

Laynie and Brittany were crazy if they thought Tommy or anyone else would ask me to prom. Lots of girls went dateless. So could I. Not a big deal.

But I wouldn't be opposed to having an escort.

My gaze darted across asphalt, past the picnic benches filled with my classmates, to Tommy. "Yeah, I'm sure I could take him. He doesn't exactly look dangerous," I said. Not with the button down shirt and glasses. Tommy might have had height on his side, but he was a little too lean. "Which means he'll bring the same emotional baggage as any other guy. Haven't met one yet who's cool with a girl being tougher than him."

"Maybe you should bulk up, so they don't feel as bad." Brittany giggled. "At least they could say it was a big, brawny girl, not a willowy short thing."

"I'm not *that* short."

"You're right." Brittany snorted and waved my words away. "I know a couple of freshmen shorter than you."

I rolled my eyes at her exaggeration. Still, I wasn't exactly a giant, which made it even harder on the guys' egos when I knocked them down. Like when Luke Pratt had taken hold of Will Mayer's pants from behind and dragged him backward across the football field. But what else was I supposed to do? Not take a stand? Screw that. Besides, it seemed wrong to let my brown belt in jujitsu go to waste when I could use it to help someone. I refused to make less of myself to please a boy. And that included Tommy — no matter how hot or sweet he was.

"Tommy seems different though," Laynie said as we watched him toss some potato chips in his mouth. "Unlike the rest of them, he's not afraid to talk to you.

Maybe he's *the guy*." She gave me a hopeful smile.

"Laynie, not everyone is looking for *the guy*," Brittany said. "Some people don't find him until they're old, like in their thirties. Right now, we're just looking for someone to take Alex to prom. That's it. He doesn't need to marry her."

Laynie's bottom lip jutted out. "No one has to get married right now. But who wouldn't want to meet *the guy* and avoid wasting possibly years kissing a bunch of duds? Oh, looks like Tommy's headed our way." She straightened in her chair.

My stomach pinched. I wouldn't admit it to Laynie or Brittany, but I had a mammoth crush on Tommy. I loved the way he talked to me as though I were one of the guys. But in a good way, like he didn't feel he had to act differently around me. On the other hand, I didn't want to be one of the guys to *him*.

"I'm not sure if he's your forever guy, Alex, but I think Laynie's right." Brittany narrowed her eyes at the approaching figure. "He definitely likes you."

Impossible. Not that I didn't think I was pretty enough, but since guys never asked me out, it was easy to assume Tommy wouldn't either. The fact that I'd shared three classes with him all year and he'd never made a move was proof enough. Maybe he just liked hanging out with me because around me was the safest place to be.

"You guys are imagining things. And would you *please* stop staring at him?" I whispered as he neared our table. When they ignored me, I nudged Brittany hard enough to start a domino effect. On Brittany's other side, Laynie jolted.

Tommy stopped right in front of me. His dark blond hair looked slightly red under the afternoon sun. "Hey."

I smiled since it was hard not to. He was just so easy to talk to. "What's up?"

He sat on the bench across from us, his hazel eyes focused on me. "Mr. Fargo's got a quiz next period. You ready for it?"

"Of course. I studied last night. You?" I asked, trying to act cool, as though I didn't want more from him than I did. My friends were suddenly silent. They had high hopes for Tommy and me, but I hated that they'd inevitably be disappointed when nothing came of it. Just like I would be.

"Yeah, I studied too." He glanced at Laynie and Brittany, then back to me. "Why don't you come sit at our table?"

For some reason, sitting with him and his friends made me want to go crawl in a hole. His guy friends could barely look me in the eye. Why would I want to sit with them *on purpose*? "We're good here," I said. "Thanks, though."

"The three prettiest girls at school and you're always by yourselves." He shook his head.

Laynie and Brittany shrugged in unison. My long, dark brown hair fell over my shoulder as my gaze dropped to the dingy plastic picnic table.

"You guys going to The Bean Pit after school?" he asked, breaking the uncomfortable silence.

"Promised my mom I'd help her bake cookies,"

Laynie said.

Brittany shook her head. "No. I have some research to do for *The Journal.* I'm the editor. I can't slack."

"Alex was just saying how she was in the mood for a cappuccino." Laynie grinned and turned to me. "Or was it hot cocoa?"

Wow, way to be obvious. Thankfully, Tommy didn't seem to notice.

"I'll buy." Tommy beamed. Not the dfopey kind of smile I'd gotten from guys who think I'm hot—until they realize I'm not fragile and helpless. His smile wasn't needy or awkward either. He was just... Tommy. A guy I could totally fall for the rest of the way—if I let myself.

"I'll drive," I offered.

"Great. Meet you in the parking lot after school?" he asked.

He'd only moved to San Diego this past fall and hadn't been around last year when I'd built my tough-girl rep. If he didn't already know about it, he'd find out soon enough. In the meantime, I'd spend some time with a guy I liked. "Sure," I said, just as the warning bell rang.

"I have to get something from my locker. See you later." His gaze swept over us, then with one more quick glance at me, he returned to his friends.

"Tommy's got it bad for you." Laynie grinned.

"He must already know about you." Brittany pursed her lips as she stared at Tommy's retreating back, then she turned to me. "Either he doesn't believe it or he doesn't care."

"If he cared about any of that, he wouldn't go through the trouble of arranging a coffee date." Laynie beamed, clearly ecstatic at the possibility that one of us could end up with a prom date.

"He's just being nice. We're friends," I said. Tommy and I may never become more than that. But I'd enjoy spending time with him, until the day he realized I'm not girlfriend material and bolted like every other guy before him. I'd probably live my whole life single and die a virgin.

~~~

The rest of the day, I obsessed on my upcoming coffee date with Tommy. Thankfully, he sat behind me in calculus, where I wouldn't be tempted to sneak peeks at him. Good thing too or I probably would've tanked the quiz and gotten one of Mr. Fargo's famous 'Fs.'

After my last class, Brittany and Laynie huddled with me by my ancient, faded blue Honda Civic, speaking in hushed voices in case Tommy snuck up on us.

"Since he's already offered, let him pay. It helps guys feel manly," Laynie said.

Brittany grasped my shoulders. "We know you can pay your own way and open the doors yourself, but if he's on it, let him do it. Just be a girl for a little while."

"I'll try, so long as I don't have to pretend to be frail so he'll like me," I said. Any minute now, Tommy would arrive and we'd go out alone, away from school and our friends. A thrill rushed through me, but I squashed it. My last date had been with Ryan who'd stopped returning my calls right after the Wes Hampton incident.

I rolled my eyes. "Like it's going to make a difference in the end."

"Maybe this time it'll work out," Laynie said, brushing a soothing hand down my arm.

"Don't get your hopes up."

"Alex," Brittany said. "We just want you to have a nice time. You deserve it."

I made my lips curve up so they wouldn't worry about me. "Thanks. You guys should get going. Don't want you two to scare him off."

"He doesn't look scared to me." Brittany nudged me with her elbow.

I followed the path of Brittany's gaze to Tommy waving from across the lot. He pointed to his backpack over his shoulder, then to his car and I nodded.

"Even if this goes nowhere and you stay friends, at least you'll have something pretty to look at." Laynie sighed.

"Would you both stop staring?" I scowled.

Brittany nudged my shoulder. "You can't blame us. He's super cute."

"True." I wiggled my fingers, hoping to shake out the tension. "Oh, hell, here he comes."

"You'll be fine." Laynie squeezed my shoulder. "He obviously likes you exactly as you are. Just roll with it."

Brittany and Laynie waved as they strolled to their own cars. I wiped my palms on my jeans and turned to face Tommy.

Chapter Two

Tommy gave me a huge grin and, for the first time, I noticed he had dimples. They made him even cuter. "You ready?" he asked.

More than. "Yeah." I reached for the handle on the driver's side to open the door, but Tommy beat me to it. I stared at him, unmoving. No guy at school had ever opened a door for me before.

"Now you're supposed to get in." A smile played on his lips.

"Thanks." I blinked, then climbed behind the wheel as he shut the door and rounded the hood. I turned the key and the engine roared to life just as he folded himself into the passenger seat. The Living Dead blared from the speakers.

"Sorry." I turned the volume knob, so I wouldn't have to strain to be heard over the music. "They're one of my favorite bands." I flashed him a smile before glancing over my shoulder and backing out of the lot.

"I even got concert tickets."

"No way. They're my favorite band too." He slapped a palm on the dashboard. "I heard they sold out the first day. You're so lucky."

I chuckled. "Not luck. I put it on my birthday wish list."

"I'll have to try that."

Or I could give him the extra ticket, since I hadn't promised it to anyone yet. Going to the concert with a huge fan would be so much more fun than taking Brittany who said she'd go but merely tolerated the music. Slim chance Tommy would still want to go with me by the time the concert date rolled around next month though. Some girl would surely snatch him up.

I cruised through the gate of the school and a mile later we rolled into the Bean Pit's parking lot.

"What time do you have to be home?" Tommy asked, opening the Bean Pit's door for me. My stomach fluttered at how sweet he was being.

"Doesn't matter. My dad's in a tournament out of town." I stopped in the coffee line. The place was packed. Tiny round tables were crammed in the overcrowded café. A few of them were people I recognized from school. I drew in a deep breath and basked in the scent of roasted coffee and vanilla.

"Right. He owns that jujitsu studio on Broadway, right?" he asked. When I only nodded, he continued, "What level belt are you?"

So he *did* know. "Brown belt. That's just below a black in jujitsu." My face flushed and I waited for Tommy to run.

His eyes bulged. "That's impressive. You worked hard for it, I'm sure."

"Yeah." I nodded, totally weirded out. He almost seemed enthusiastic over my skills.

"That is so cool. Bet you don't have to worry about walking down dark alleys late at night." He grinned.

I snorted. "Very funny. Actually, I think most people wish I didn't go to their school. Like I upset the natural order of things."

"I heard that you single-handedly cleaned up our school. One bully can terrorize a lot of kids. I'd say there are more people happy to have you there than not."

"I guess so," I said, staring at my feet.

"How old were you when you got your first lesson?" he asked as though girls like me were as natural as oxygen.

"Five," I answered, hope sparking in me for that second date.

"That means you've been training for thirteen years. Wow."

I laughed. "Yes, but school and sleepovers kept me from training a lot."

We stepped up to the counter and ordered, then waited at the other end. He reached in front of me to get a stir stick, which brought his face inches from mine. He smelled of mint and soap. He was close enough that I'd only have to lean forward just a hair and our lips would touch. They were nice lips too. Full, but not too big. Very kissable.

Stir stick in hand, Tommy withdrew and leaned against the counter to observe the other patrons in the coffee house. I followed suit, noting Wes Hampton, San Diego High's class ass, sitting at the other end of the room in an animated conversation with a couple friends. The same guy I'd made an example of last year.

I'd never have to worry about him again, but his presence only reminded me of who I was. My coffee date with Tommy was a joke and I was just as crazy as my friends if I thought it could work with us. I shouldn't have come.

A barista called our names and set our drinks on the counter. We each grabbed our cup and headed for the only empty table.

"Thanks for the hot chocolate," I said once we'd both sat.

"Thanks for the ride." Tommy grinned, then he grew sober. His palms wrapped around the steaming paper cup. I liked his hands. They weren't all soft and pasty, like he never got them dirty. "You live with your dad, right? What happened to your mom?" He stilled. "I'm sorry. Maybe I shouldn't have brought that up."

"It's okay. She died when I was one, so I don't remember her at all." I tasted my cocoa.

"What happened to her?" he asked, sampling his cappuccino.

"Mugging gone wrong. That was when my dad started studying martial arts. He wanted to be able to protect me like he couldn't do for my mom."

"And he taught you too, so you could take care of yourself when he wasn't around?" Tommy asked.

I nodded and took another sip of my drink, letting the sweet, hot cocoa warm me. Whether it was the company, the drink or the dimples, I felt more relaxed than I had in ages. Tommy was good for me. Even if he never became my boyfriend, he'd be a great friend.

I was suddenly slammed forward and cocoa sloshed in my cup. I set it on the table and spun in my chair to see who'd crashed into me. Wes Hampton stared down at me. "Wh—" I froze at the expression on Wes's face. Pure hatred.

He looked me right in the eye, leaned over and nudged a corner of the table. Without me holding my cup, it toppled and liquid spilled out, dripping over the edge of the table and onto my knee.

I shot out of my seat. "What the hell?"

Tommy's chair scraped against the floor as he rose too. I hoped he would stay there, out of the way, in case things got ugly. "Wes, what are you doing?" he asked, scowling.

Ignoring Tommy, Wes sneered and pushed out his chest, making him seem even taller.

"Some manners would be nice." I pointed to the wet mess on the floor.

"Guess you need to clean it up, huh? Or are you going to cry like a girl first?"

Maybe he was drunk, though I couldn't think how he'd managed to drink since school had only just let out. I studied him a moment, looking for a sign, but he seemed sober enough. Same with his two friends.

"Wes, what the hell is wrong with you?" Tommy said, standing at my side.

"Yeah, what's your problem?" I shifted and turned to make myself a smaller target, my limbs on standby to strike.

"As if you don't know. I've seen you all over school acting like you own it, telling people what to do. You're not tough. You're just a stupid girl who needs to be put in her place." Wes snickered and his friends echoed him.

"Walk away, Wes," I said. Was he on steroids or something and that's how he figured he'd take me in a fight? If so, could I handle him and his friends if they were all amped up, while still shielding Tommy? I stretched my shoulders back, bringing my eyes level to his wide chest.

"Listen to the girl," Tommy urged.

"This is none of your business." Wes glared at Tommy, then his brown eyes fixed on mine. "You're not the only one who's been getting karate lessons, Alex."

Tommy moved to get in front of me and I gave him a warning look. "Tommy, I got this."

If Wes was on some kind of drug and I didn't do well, I still had a better chance than Tommy. And I really didn't want Wes messing up my favorite café. "Maybe we should go outside."

"I'd love nothing more." Wes flashed me a cocky smile and headed out the door.

I moved to follow, but Tommy grabbed my arm.

"And I'm supposed to just stand here while you guys go at it?" Tommy's hazel eyes burned into mine.

"You're kidding, right?"

"I forgot you two are friends," I said. "I'll try not to hurt him, okay?"

He blinked, still gripping my arm. "I helped him with English Lit. That doesn't make us friends. And anyway, that's not the point."

"You're afraid I'm the one who'll get hurt? I can take care of myself."

"Against three guys?" Tommy lifted one brow and eyed me.

"I beat him once, so now he has something to prove. Better to deal with it now than in some dark alley. You should stay inside." I twisted out of his grasp, whirled around and headed outside to the waiting bully.

I pushed open the door and the bells tied to the handle chimed. A cool breeze greeted me and my long hair tickled my neck. All the parking spots were full and there were a handful of people either getting out of their cars in front of the store next door or moving toward the parking lot. And then there were the coffee house patrons who could easily see us from the other side of the large window. If things went my way, Wes was in for another public humiliation. Hopefully, it wouldn't come to that. If it did though, maybe Wes would learn from it and this would be the last time.

He spotted me and straightened, a smug look on his face.

"You sure you want to do this?" I eyed his friends warily, hoping they didn't plan to jump in. I heard Tommy's steps behind me, but I didn't take my eyes off Wes or his goons.

"You're not going to hit a girl, Wes," Tommy said.

Wes scoffed. "She's not a girl."

Oh, God. "Tommy, stay out of this," I said.

Tommy ignored my request and stepped in front of me. "She *looks* like a girl to me."

"Well, when she starts *acting* like a girl, I'll start treating her like one." Wes sneered.

"Sure, you do that." Tommy nodded solemnly. "But you'll have to go through me."

Wes snickered. "You're willing to get your ass beat for *her*?"

"I'd hate to see you do something you'll regret the rest of your life," Tommy said.

Wes gave Tommy a smug look. "And why would I regret it?"

"Maybe because you'll go down in history as the guy who hit a girl. More likely, you'll become infamous for getting beat up *by* a girl. You can kiss your social life goodbye, along with any dates you might've had." Tommy folded his arms over his chest and lifted his chin.

"Whatever. I'm bored with her anyway." Wes narrowed his eyes. "You'd be more fun to fight."

"Not really." Tommy held up a hand. "I don't give up easily."

Wes studied Tommy a moment, then his gaze darted to me for an instant before his arm pulled back. He threw a fist toward Tommy and I stepped between them. With my right hand, I hit the inside of Wes's elbow, then struck his neck with the side of my other hand. Wes yelped and jumped back, staring at me with wide eyes. His two friends inched backward, putting distance between me and them.

Wes turned to his friends. "Y-you guys ready to go?" he asked.

And just like that, Wes and his friends made a dash for their car. I kept my eyes on them until they drove away, then whirled around to Tommy, my hands balling into fists. "I could've handled them without you."

"I know that," Tommy growled. "But you shouldn't *have* to."

"But I *do* have to. You could've gotten hurt."

"You think that's worse than watching them try to take you down? I don't think so." His jaw tightened. "Look, I know you're tough and you can handle them. But I can't stand by and watch them hit you. I just can't. And maybe you don't care, but I do."

My jaw dropped and my fists unfurled. "I was betting that they couldn't hurt me and I was right."

He inched closer and gently took my hand. "Bodily harm has nothing to do with it. You're still a girl and someone needs to look out for you in that way."

So he was worried what would happen to... what... my feminine psyche? More shocking, he was *still there*—and holding my hand.

I'd had it all wrong, thinking I needed a guy to be tougher than me. What I really needed was someone to safeguard the part I put aside to fight. The girl in me.

And that guy was definitely Tommy—who seemed happy to take me on. But I had to ask, just to make sure. "And you're the guy for the job?"

"Well... yeah."

"Okay." My lips curled up. "What else does the job entail?"

"For starters, when you need a date, you can use me," he said, grinning.

I tilted my head thoughtfully. "Hmm... does that include prom?"

"I'd love to go with you. Thanks for asking." He chuckled. "Under one condition: *I* will take *you* to prom, not the other way around. Meaning I'll pick you up and take care of everything."

My smile widened. "Deal."

"Hypothetically speaking," Tommy lowered his voice to a whisper and tugged on my hand to bring me closer, "if I was going to kiss you, would I be risking life and limb?"

"You wait until *now* to worry about your limbs?" I laughed as my arms circled his waist. "Why weren't you worried about them before?"

Tommy cradled my face in both hands. "Because I was only thinking of you," he said just before his lips touched mine.

The End

Singled Out

Veronica Blade

Chapter One

I squirmed on the bench between my two best friends, Laynie and Alex, as they waxed poetic about fixing me up. Seriously, their matchmaking attempts had ruined my appetite for the bean and beef burrito on the table in front of me — and that's saying a lot. Usually I could chow down Mexican food, day or night.

"Oh, come on, Brittany. You can't tell me there's not one dateable guy in the whole school." Laynie pressed a hand against her forehead to shield her eyes from the noon sun and scanned the school grounds.

I followed Laynie's gaze to the seniors spilled out onto the steps of the school entrance. Others sat on the low wall nearby or sprawled across the lawn in small cliques. "Uhm, actually, I can," I said, digging my English Lit notes from my backpack. If I wasn't going to eat, I could use the time for homework, which would free me up later to finish my article for the school newspaper. "Besides, none of the guys here seem interested in me."

"Brittany, Brittany, Brittany." Alex blew long, dark brown bangs out of her eyes. "Everyone knows you're the reason the debate team killed at regional. The guys are intimidated by you and afraid they'll never win an argument. Just because they might need a little encouragement doesn't mean they don't think you're hot."

Laynie nodded. "Exactly. You have the three Bs: Blond. Boobs. Brains. Although for most guys here, the third is optional."

Truer words were never spoken.

"Why would I go anywhere with a guy who finds the third optional?" I shoved my untouched tray aside, whipped out a pencil and paused to steal a quick glance across the grassy field, past a sprinkling of other lunch tables, to the back of Wyatt's head of shaggy brown hair. He was leaning against a tree, talking with several of his friends. My stomach fluttered.

Just then, Josie—the reason Wyatt and I had broken up—strolled by the guys, tossing her long, silky auburn hair and flashing them a sultry you-know-I'm-hot smile. One of the nearby jocks wolf whistled and a chorus of cat calls ensued. I couldn't see Wyatt's face, but I guessed he was watching her too. Any time Josie strutted around in a short skirt with those long legs exposed, even the girls looked. She was all golden skin and radiant smiles. And she'd made-out with nearly every cute guy in San Diego High's senior class.

Laynie scowled, her green eyes glued to Josie as she

held a cup of juice just below her lips. "Why do guys go for girls like that?"

"Hormones," Alex said, waving a french fry at Laynie. "But there's still some good ones who want a real girlfriend. Like my Tommy." Her gaze met his a few yards away at another table and they exchanged a smile. He rose from the bench and headed our way.

Tommy stopped at our table, but remained standing. "Just talked to a friend from my old school who wants to take you to prom, Britt."

Heat crept up my neck. Alex and Laynie — and now Tommy — were acting as if I were incapable of getting a date without help. Could I be that undesirable? Regardless, I found their intrusiveness humiliating.

"I'm fine with going to prom stag. Laynie and Alex are done playing cupid, Tommy. You can come sit with us again."

"He understands I'm on a mission and his banishment is just temporary," Alex said to me, then switched to him. "Babe, tell us about the guy from your old school."

"Please don't." I inwardly groaned and lifted my chin. "Alex, I'm happy for you guys, but I don't need a serious relationship right now."

"Did I say you had to marry him?" Alex asked. "Don't pretend like you don't want a prom date."

"I'll let you guys work it out. See you after school, babe." He leaned over and dropped a kiss on the top of her head, then turned to leave.

Alex flashed him a smile, then continued her search

for eligible prospects as she munched another fry.

I shot Alex and Laynie a stern look, then picked up my burrito. I needed to eat, whether I wanted to or not, if I was going to keep up my strength against their meddling.

When I chomped down, the other end of my burrito burst open and filled my lap with grayish-brown beans and chunks of beef.

"Gross." Laynie grimaced, handing me a napkin.

I sighed as I took the napkin and scooped up the blob, but the fabric of my jeans had already absorbed the greasy mush. I couldn't go the rest of the day slathered in burrito slime. So far, my day was just peachy.

"Gotta go clean up. See you guys after school." I gathered my belongings, then stormed toward the bathroom.

As I ran water over paper towels, tears filled my eyes. Not because my friends were interfering in my love life, but because I knew that Wyatt, the guy I really wanted to go to prom with, would never ask me. Even if he did, I'd have to say no.

After serious rubbing, the stain was history, but my pants were soaked. If only the burrito guts had landed closer to my knees. But, no, it just *had* to hit my upper thigh. Now I'd have to walk the long corridor, past my classmates, looking like I'd peed my pants. Just great.

My eyes burned in frustration as I swung the bathroom door open, hoping to get to my locker for a sweater to tie around my waist. Just as I cleared the doorway, I crashed into a hard body and grunted.

"Whoa." Strong arms flashed to my waist to steady

me. "You okay?" Wyatt asked in that low, sexy voice that always made me melt.

I blinked, nodded and told myself that I hated him.

"You sure?"

"Don't I look fine?" I dropped my gaze to his shoulder. If he looked into my eyes, he might see that I wasn't okay at all.

"You *always* look fine," he said, dropping his hands from my waist. The smile in his voice ranked about a nine on the flirt-o-meter. I looked up to see his mouth curved into a smile that caused my stomach to flip. "You took off so fast, I thought something was wrong," he said.

He'd been watching and came looking for me? Doubtful since he hadn't wanted anything from me all year. More likely, Wyatt being there had nothing to do with me. Just a coincidence. I mean, why would he start caring now?

"I'm eating challenged." I waved a hand at my wet jeans, then remembered he and his friends had been talking to Josie just before the burrito fiasco. "I'm amazed you had time to notice. You looked kinda busy with Josie."

As soon as the words were out, I regretted them. Why couldn't I just leave it alone? Oh, yeah, because I hadn't gotten over him.

He blew out a breath. "A year later and you're still stuck on her?"

"Well, she's the reason we broke up." I threw my hands up in surrender.

"No, *you're* the reason we broke up." He rocked back

on his heels, arms folded over his chest.

I gritted my teeth. Had he expected me to just stand by while she slutted herself all over him? But I refused to reveal I'd witnessed them kissing. Letting him know how much he had hurt me would only add to the humiliation of his cheating on me in the first place.

Worse, once he knew that I knew, he had no reason to keep quiet about it. I'd learned the hard way that nothing was sacred in school and people could be mean. I'd rather be known by the entire school as the girl who dumped Wyatt than overhear whispers of how I hadn't been enough for him so he'd turned to Josie.

Students were strolling past us, staring. The warning bell would sound soon and we'd both have to hightail it to class. But until then, I was in the mood for a fight.

"How do you figure it's my fault?" I raised my chin. "I wasn't the one flirting with her."

"There's a difference between talking and flirting. One day, when you're older, maybe you'll get that." He'd abandoned the playful tone in favor of a little bite.

My fists balled at my sides, knowing his crimes went deeper than just flirting. "Yeah, well, Josie talks with her *hands*. You seriously couldn't expect me to be okay with another girl plastering herself all over you."

"Major exaggeration. If you knew me at all, you'd *know* I wasn't trying to hook up with her. What was I supposed to do, not talk to another girl for no reason? It would've been rude."

I took a deep breath, then softened my voice. "Not

stopping her was as good as encouraging her."

Wyatt's brows drew together as if that were a new concept to him.

"Then you took her to prom." I chewed off the last word, my jaw clenched.

"You told me to piss off and she asked me." His voice rose in volume. "Was I supposed to go to prom *alone* after you dumped me?"

I'd broken it off with him as a last resort, expecting him to fight for me, hoping he'd volunteer some kind of explanation for kissing her. I sagged against the wall and rubbed my temples, fighting the tears I'd never let him see.

"If you'd made it clear to Josie you were taken, we probably wouldn't have broken up." A full year later and we were rehashing the same old crap and it didn't sting any less. What was the point?

A moment later, the bell rang and I darted past him. But I really wanted to retreat into the bathroom and hide until my jeans dried. Actually, I wanted to go straight home until my hands no longer trembled and my heart stopped aching.

~~~

The next day during lunch at our usual table outside, Alex and Laynie played another round of Pimping Brittany — much to my irritation.

"What about Aiden?" Laynie brushed a lock of curly, red hair out of her eyes and nodded toward a group of guys beyond Tommy.

I followed her gaze, focusing on Aiden. "Too emo. I can't date a guy who wears his jeans tighter than I do."

On my other side, Alex tapped a short, unpolished fingernail on her bottom lip. "Kyle?"

"Seriously?" I stirred my yogurt. "He's never not stoned. Can you imagine *me* dating a guy who can't stay sober long enough to pass his driver's test?" I shuddered.

"Who then? There must be someone you've been secretly obsessing on." Alex sighed and turned away. A moment later, her head whipped around with a huge grin. "Wyatt."

I commanded my eyes not to go left, but they defied me and shot to Wyatt's profile. My pulse quickened.

"Just as gorgeous as ever, right?" Laynie raised one brow. "You're not going to try to deny he's still a catch, are you?"

"Wouldn't dream of it, but you guys already know he's not into me — never was." Not enough anyway. I dragged my eyes from Wyatt and feigned indifference, swallowing a spoonful of yogurt.

"I was just joking. But now that I see you protest too much, I'm beginning to wonder." Alex narrowed her eyes at me and scooted closer. "Maybe the reason you go out of your way to avoid him is because you still like him."

I snorted. "Believe what you want. Even if I did like him — which I don't — he's not interested."

"How do you know?" Laynie lifted a shoulder. "You dumped him before he ever got a chance to kiss you. For all we know, he totally regrets cheating on you and wants you back."

"You've been reading too many romance novels." Butterflies waged war in my stomach as I scooped another bite from the yogurt container. Yeah, sure, a big part of me — all of me actually — was hoping he might secretly want me back. Even if he still held any remnants of affinity for me, after my outburst the day before, there's no way he'd consider me now. Besides, I'd never trust him knowing that anytime a girl came on to him, he wouldn't want to be *rude*.

"I think..." Laynie tilted her head, studying me.

Uh-oh. Fingers of fear licked the nape of my neck at the possibility of them trying to set me up with Wyatt. "What?"

"Maybe he had a logical explanation for kissing Josie. I've always said that."

I snorted, my hope deflating that anything good would come from the conversation. "Right. Like his lips slipped and she happened to be there."

Laynie rolled her eyes. "You never even gave him a chance to defend himself."

"Doesn't matter. It's been a year and he's long over it. Besides, he's not my type," I lied.

Alex wiggled her eyebrows. "Have you seen Wyatt dance? He's every girl's type. Besides, it's just prom, not a lifelong commitment. We need to triple date."

Oh, yeah, I'd seen Wyatt dance. Watching his moves made me want to stuff dollar bills into his waistband — and anywhere else I could fit my hands. But almost anyone could learn to dance well if they practiced enough. That wasn't what drew me to him.

Wyatt wasn't a douche, like one of those guys who got popular by intimidating everyone in his path. He earned my crush when he'd driven me to Planned Parenthood to do research on safe sex for an article I'd been writing. How many guys would go *there* for a girl when he hadn't even kissed her yet? And when he'd invited me over for dinner to meet his family and I'd seen how sweet he was to his baby brother, I'd fallen for him even harder.

I'd never forget the Wyatt I'd known then — or thought I'd known — the Wyatt before *Josie* had come along. But I needed someone loyal and refused to settle for less. "I don't need a prom date. I'm serious. Besides, Laynie doesn't have a date either. Why am I being singled out?"

The next instant, afs if I had no control over my eyeballs, they shot to Wyatt who was standing and high-fiving a couple of his friends. His gaze met mine, paused for a split second, then he turned and sat again with his back to me. He probably thought I was pathetic for staring at him. Brittany, the stalker. Whatever.

"Oh, my God! Did you see that, Alex?" Laynie's hand flew to her mouth. "She still *likes* him."

Alex whipped around and narrowed her eyes at me.

Oh, no. I'd seen that determined look in their eyes before. When those two teamed up, nothing could stop them. I was in so much trouble.

Chapter Two

"*No, I definitely* don't like Wyatt anymore. Not in that way," I lied again, but my face heated.

"I can't believe we missed it this whole time." Laynie giggled, completely ignoring my denial. "We have some work to do, Alex."

"We sure do." Alex fist-bumped Laynie.

I swallowed quickly. "No. Would you guys just drop it already?" My words came out squeaky.

"Wyatt seems like one of the good guys. And he was so into you. Cheating on you just doesn't fit." Alex's big brown eyes narrowed as if her devious mind was hitting overdrive.

Laynie nodded. "I've always said that. Why does nobody listen to me?"

"Oh, I don't know." My brows drew together. "Maybe because I witnessed it personally?"

"He hasn't been serious about anyone since Britt,"

Alex said as if I didn't exist, her gaze drifting back to him.

"That we know of. Maybe he has a girlfriend from another school." I shrugged. "Doesn't matter. I'm done with him," I stated with finality.

When they didn't comment, my head snapped to Laynie first, then to Alex. They were both staring at Wyatt.

I bit my bottom lip. "You know what? Now that I think about it, Aiden would make the perfect prom date. Make it happen, girls. I'm in."

"And let you settle for a guy you don't like? Not on your life." Laynie gave me a sympathetic smile.

Even if he'd learned to be faithful, it's not as if Wyatt would ever like me again. Now that he knew I was still hanging onto all that anger, he probably thought I was a jealous psycho. Maybe he was right. Maybe if I'd been more understanding... maybe if I'd let him handle Josie in his own way...

But I hadn't. And even as I wished I'd done things differently that night when I'd arrived at The Bean Pit to meet Wyatt — just in time to see Josie pressed against him with her hands cupping his face and her mouth melding with his — I knew I wouldn't change a thing. I'd still quietly slip away and let him think he'd been stood up. Then I'd avoid him at school, just like I did back then. I hadn't wanted to hear his excuses for kissing Josie and still don't. Because cheating is betrayal, no matter how pretty the paper my friends use to wrap it up or what kind of bow they stick on it.

I stole a peek at Wyatt across the lawn. He looked

deep in conversation with Colin and was shaking his head. "I'm going to prom alone."

"So that's it? You're just giving up?" Laynie stared at me with wide, sad eyes.

"It's not giving up if you were never going for it in the first place." I looked at my two friends pointedly and they exchanged frowns. "I'm doing a summer internship at the newspaper and in the fall I'll start college. Maybe one day, I'll meet a great guy. Until then, I don't need the hassle."

"You," Alex thrust an index finger at me, "are not right in the head. I mean, who graduates high school without ever kissing a guy?"

That was one of my biggest regrets — that I'd been so slow with Wyatt. I couldn't believe such a hot, sexy guy would choose me over every other girl. So I'd put him off. Instead of giving up on me, he'd stayed after school with me to do sketches for the newspaper.

After a few weeks and one impromptu dinner with his family when I'd driven him home, I'd finally said yes to a coffee date. Just when I'd decided to let myself love him, Josie had swooped in. But I couldn't turn back time and dwelling on it wouldn't help me move on with my life. "It's *my* choice. If I want to get my master's degree on schedule, I can't let myself be thrown off track." I swallowed the last spoonful of my yogurt.

"That's eons away, Britt." Laynie shook her head. "You can't live without love. It's not right."

"People do it all the time," I chirped, setting my

spoon down. "You guys should leave Wyatt out of it. You'll only make things worse."

Laynie inched closer to make sure she had my attention, then lowered her voice. "When the guy you love isn't speaking to you, how much worse can it get?"

Oh, he was speaking to me alright, except now we were further apart than ever. But I didn't want to tell them about our heated words the day before. Thankfully, I wouldn't see Wyatt again until Monday. I had all weekend to get over it.

Alex pursed her lips and let her gaze wander. As soon as Colin and Wyatt had strolled by us and through the double doors, she huddled close to Laynie and me. "My dad's at another jujitsu tournament this weekend, so I'm all alone. Party at my house Saturday night. Nothing too crazy. Just a small get-together. Maybe you'll meet someone else and get a prom date, Britt."

"We're not still on my love life, are we?" I slumped on the bench. "Fine. Just make sure you don't invite Wyatt and I'll be there."

"Deal." Alex held up her hands. "Not one peep from us to Wyatt."

~~~

Saturday, my paranoia kicked in. What if Alex and Laynie were still scheming and had figured out a way around their promise? A loophole. The very thought of them succeeding at orchestrating a face-to-face with Wyatt made my stomach knot.

I'd planned to distract myself all day with a movie or a book until the last possible minute, but Laynie picked me up early to help Alex get ready for the mini-party. If I'd been on top of things, I would've bailed as soon as I saw her. But I didn't want to break my word. Still, what if Wyatt found out about the party somehow and showed up uninvited?

As I helped rearrange furniture and set out snacks, wondering if Wyatt would waltz in at any second kept my adrenaline racing and my veins humming.

With only moments before showtime, my stomach twisted as I snatched up my duffle bag and dashed into the bathroom to get ready. I spent more time than usual on my hair, straightening it and then doing my makeup, just in case Wyatt showed up. If he saw me in the short, black skirt and low cut, sleeveless top talking to some other guy, preferably a cute one, I'd make sure *I* was the one ignoring *him*. Then, maybe he'd be sorry for breaking my heart.

By eight-thirty, not only had nearly all our guests arrived, but a few extras I'd never met. A couple of the new guys were kind of cute.

As Alex's living room filled, the noise level rose. When the voices drowned out the music, Alex cranked it up until the wood floor vibrated from the bass, enticing a few couples to dance.

We hadn't anticipated so many people and I was grateful no one had brought any booze—that we knew of. Not that I had particularly strong feelings against alcohol but I'd been to a few parties where the house had been trashed after the partiers got wasted. My parents were friends with Alex's dad, so if she got nailed, so would I.

Still no Colin or Wyatt in sight. One of the new guys had glanced my way more than once. I was beginning to think the party was a brilliant idea after all.

Once everyone knew the house rules—like staying out of her dad's room and no smoking inside—I snagged a soda, leaned against Alex's kitchen counter and scanned the faces in the crowd. Just as I took a gulp, Colin walked through the front door—with Wyatt right behind him. I coughed when liquid went down the wrong pipe. As my lungs burned and struggled to eject the foreign substance, I noticed Wyatt in my peripheral vision. Watching me.

Just great. Fighting the flush creeping into my cheeks, I spun around and grabbed a paper towel to wipe my eyes. I searched the vicinity for moral support, but my two best friends were talking to him. Traitors.

"Wyatt!" a girl screamed, grabbing his hand. She was pretty with straight black hair that fell to her shoulders and beautiful brown eyes lined with thick lashes. And a body made for dancing.

He laughed as she dragged him onto the makeshift dance floor, but he didn't resist. I watched him move to the thrumming of the bass, envying the girl for being so close to him.

I wasn't the only one watching Wyatt. A quick glance around the room told me that more than half the girls in the room were admiring his moves. Okay, they were admiring more than his moves, but I didn't want to ponder what the oglers were thinking. Because I no longer had a right to speculate on his love life and would probably never have that right again.

He'd gotten a haircut since I'd seen him at school. It was still messy, but in a sexy way, like he'd taken time for mousse. And his t-shirt and jeans were missing the signature holes, as if he'd put some thought into his wardrobe. He'd never looked hotter.

The song finished, then drifted into a ballad. Wyatt smiled at the black-haired girl and shook his head, then rejoined Colin. Alex resumed the tour, coaxing the guys through the living room. As they headed my way into the kitchen to the drink cooler, I slipped away into the living room.

Wiping my sweaty palms on my skirt, I leaned against the counter, the kitchen behind me. I wondered what the chances were of one of those cute guys appearing in the next few seconds, falling all over me and making Wyatt regret the day he'd cheated on me.

I felt a hand on my shoulder and turned hopefully...

"Wyatt looks good tonight," Laynie said with a grin. "Aren't you glad he came?"

Yeah, about that... I scowled. "No and I can't believe you guys invited him. How could you?"

Laynie blinked, then gave me a wide-eyed innocent look. "We didn't. I swear."

Though I believed her, I suspected she wasn't completely clueless. "Then how did he get here?"

She hesitated a moment, biting her lip. "I guess Tommy feels like he owes you."

"What?" My mouth dropped open.

"You have selective memory. You and I helped with Alex and Tommy, and that worked out. You didn't think meddling was such a bad idea at the time." Her mouth curved into a mischievous smile, then she glanced over my shoulder. "Be right back."

As annoyed as I wanted to be with Tommy, Laynie had a point. I had no right to complain. Lost in my own nightmare, I didn't notice when she returned. She flipped a thumb toward the kitchen. "We should mingle."

But Wyatt was in there, just on the other side of the counter. Next to him, Alex tossed a potato chip in her mouth, then curled her index finger at us. Before I could protest, Laynie tugged on my arm. "Let's go see what Alex wants," she said.

Laynie and Alex had to be up to something. If I resisted going in with Laynie, I'd attract more attention. I groaned inwardly when she led me away.

As we neared Alex, Colin's hand shot out to stop Laynie. "Hey, where's the bathroom?"

"I can show you," she told Colin, then turned to me with a smile. "Stay right here. I won't be long."

Somehow, I'd ended up standing right in front of Wyatt, so close we were almost touching. I cast a quick glance around the room, searching the faces of our guests to discover Alex had vanished. Rather than stand there like a loser, I took a deep breath and forced the corners of my mouth up. "Hi."

"Hey, Britt." Wyatt shoved his hands in his pockets. Instead of returning my smile, his gaze lowered to the floor.

But he hadn't bolted. Yet.

"Uhm." Things may never again be perfect with Wyatt, but maybe things could be *better*. Maybe we could at least be friends and I'd have some part of him. "I'm sorry about the other day. I shouldn't have gotten so worked up."

He gave a careless shrug. "Yeah, well, I shouldn't have taken Josie to prom."

Wow. Progress. But did he also realize he shouldn't have kissed her? I narrowed my eyes to prod him into doing better.

"I only went with her because you blew me off. Then Robby said he was taking you."

Anger welled up again. He still wasn't admitting what he'd done. "But that doesn't solve the earlier problem."

He growled and rolled his eyes. "Will you give it a rest? Why can't we just agree to disagree?"

I shook my head, my jaw tightening. Sucking in a deep, calming breath, I vowed to make him understand. "If you were in my place and Robby was all over me, wouldn't you have been pissed? And if you'd seen me kiss Robby," I slowed my words for dramatic effect, "you totally would've stood me up, too."

I studied him a moment, waiting for his admission. Instead, his mouth dropped open, but he didn't say anything. He just stared, first at me, then his toes. Then, without another word, he pivoted and left.

Tears stung my eyes. I'd laid it all out and he still didn't apologize — and he probably never would. A faint throb began at my temples, threatening to morph into a migraine. Suddenly, I just wanted to go home.

Alex and Laynie magically appeared, flanking me.

"What did he say?" Laynie asked.

"Were you nice to him?" Alex hissed.

I bristled. "Yes. And you saw what happened."

"For a second there, it looked promising," Laynie said, pouting.

I sighed. "Told you it was hopeless. Tommy shouldn't have invited him."

Alex's brows furrowed in confusion. "I really thought Wyatt was into you. When Tommy talked to Colin — "

"Colin's involved, too?" I clenched my jaw to keep from shouting.

"We had to find out if Wyatt already had a date for prom. He doesn't. But it's obvious we'll have to reassess the situation."

"There is no situation. Except that he's still the same old Wyatt and you both just rubbed my face in it. So, thank you very much for taking my misery to a higher level." I checked my watch, the need to get away nearly overpowering me. "My mom's dragging me out of bed super early tomorrow. I should get going."

Alex rolled her eyes while Laynie stuck out her bottom lip.

"At least you guys are talking. That's progress,"

Laynie said.

Not if he didn't regret what he'd done. "I know you two meant well, but you can't force this. I'll call you tomorrow."

"Brittany, wait." Laynie grabbed my hand. "Maybe he just needs more time."

He'd had almost a year to reflect on all the ways he'd screwed up. "He's not getting more time. And you two are backing off." I longed for a hole to crawl into.

"Okay, fine," Alex said, folding her arms over her chest.

"Wait. I drove and no way am I letting you walk almost a mile in the dark." Still holding my hand, Laynie gave it a squeeze. "Hang on. I'll get my purse."

She released me and I made a beeline to the front door. I stepped outside, the crisp night air tickling my cheeks.

Alex's front door slammed just as I stepped off the porch and landed on the narrow path that divided the lawn. Assuming Laynie was right behind me, I continued walking toward her car across the street.

"Brittany!"

My breath hitched at Wyatt's voice.

Chapter Three

Just before reaching the curb, I spun to face Wyatt. "Yeah?"

"You're leaving?"

I nodded, feeling totally defeated and wondering why he wanted to know.

He quickly closed the distance, from the steps to the curb, stopping in front of me. "I was wondering... uh... I was thinking maybe you'd like to get some coffee," he said. "I've been thinking about what you said earlier and thought maybe we could talk. Like... talk. Not argue."

I stared at him wide-eyed, my stomach twisting into knots. "Now?"

"Yeah." He exhaled. "The Bean Pit's still open. I'll drive."

Stunned, I managed to close my mouth. It's not like he'd admitted to kissing Josie. Nor had he given an excuse yet for his actions. But he'd followed me out wanting to talk and I couldn't make myself tell him no. "Okay."

He flicked a thumb toward his old, faded green Camaro. "I'm right here."

On the way to his car, I looked back at the house. Laynie stood halfway through the front door wearing a huge grin. I waved to her, then climbed inside Wyatt's car.

I didn't want to have any deep conversations without his full attention, so I held my tongue, my eyes sweeping across the Camaro's faded, cracked dashboard and the naked, metal ceiling. He'd bussed tables at Dino's Pizza since I could remember and had mentioned he'd been saving up for a car. Then we'd stopped talking. When I'd seen him cruise into the school lot one morning, secretly I'd been proud of him.

"Classic," I said, waving my hand to indicate the car.

He flashed a grin. "I almost have enough money for a paint job. Then I'll fix the dash and ceiling."

I had no doubt that Wyatt would accomplish anything he set his mind to. "It's clean, too," I said, noting the lack of dirt or garbage on the floor. "So unguy-like. Impressive."

He chuckled and pulled into the parking lot of The Bean Pit.

Wyatt swung open the front door to the coffee house and the scent of pastries and roasted coffee beans rushed me. As we made our way to the line, I nibbled on a fingernail and waited for him to start the conversation. He obviously had something to say or he wouldn't have invited me out. The suspense was killing me.

We bellied up to the counter and ordered our drinks.

When the cashier told us the amount, I reached into my purse, but Wyatt thrust a ten-dollar bill at her.

"Thanks," I told him.

"No problem." He took his change from the cashier, stuffed a dollar into the tip jar, and motioned toward the end of the counter where we waited for our drinks. He threw me a smile, then averted his gaze.

I couldn't read him at all, but at least he wasn't ignoring me. Until he spilled what was on his mind and put me out of my misery, more small talk seemed like a good idea. "What do you plan to major in next year?" I asked.

"Graphic design. Eventually, I'll get into computer-generated imagery."

"That's awesome," I said. "You always were a good artist. I still have that picture you drew of Alex and me."

"Are you still writing?"

I lifted one shoulder. "When I can. Mostly, just the articles for the school newspaper."

"That's cool."

"Thank you," I told the barista, picking up my latte. I scooted Wyatt's black coffee toward him and turned to search the crowded room for an empty table. Nothing.

"I saw a spot outside." He shot to the door, opened it for me and waited for me to walk through.

We sat at a rickety metal table at the opposite end of the patio, claiming chairs across from each other. Dried coffee spills marred the surface and a lone stir stick lay abandoned.

Wyatt stared blankly into his paper cup, then took a sip from it.

"You cut your hair. Short," I said, just to fill the awkward silence.

He ran a hand over his head. "Too short?"

"No. Looks good." Everything about him looked good. I found myself wanting to *touch* him. Crap.

"I was growing it out, but my mom bribed me into getting rid of it."

"What was the bribe?"

"New tires for my car."

"Score," I said, trying not to sound too enthusiastic since he hadn't made things right with me yet.

"Yeah." He grinned, as if we'd never been estranged. "Maybe when it gets long again, I can negotiate a paint job."

"Devious." A smile snuck onto my face before I could stop it. Lord, I'd missed him.

His gaze strayed to his coffee cup again before focusing on me. "Are you sticking around for the summer or do you have plans?"

"Both. After graduation, I have an internship at *The Daily Journal.* I'll be busy." I didn't want him to think I had no life without him. I had a life... just a hole in my heart to go along with it. "How about you?"

"I'll get a summer job, then go to a local college in the fall so I can keep an eye on my mom. I don't like her being alone."

"That's nice of you to stay in town for her," I said.

He nodded. "You're right, you know."

"About what?" I wasn't sure what we were talking about.

"Everything."

I narrowed my eyes. "Everything? Can you be a little more specific?"

"Yeah. I totally would've pummeled Robby if he'd hit on you while we were together. I wasn't looking at it from your perspective at all. I figured since I wasn't interested in Josie, you should just trust me."

"I *did* trust you." Until I caught him kissing Josie, that is. "But you weren't encouraging her to stop flirting."

"I get it now." He met my gaze. "But, at the time, I felt bad for her."

"Wait. I was the one upset, but you felt bad for *her?*" I hissed.

He stared me down. "Let me finish."

I rolled my eyes and mimed zipping my lips.

"I was trying to let her down easy. She's flirty, yeah, but I thought if I made it obvious to everyone I was into you, she'd give up."

"But in the end, you took her to prom and hooked up with her anyway. If you really liked me, you wouldn't have done that." I held my breath and waited for his response, my body frozen in place.

"I took her to prom, yeah. Because you'd stood me up for our date. Then I drove her home, but I didn't even kiss her goodnight." He eyed the liquid in his cup.

My eyebrows rose. "But why not hook up with her? You and I weren't together anymore." And it's not like he hadn't already kissed her.

"Because you were the one I wanted to be with. And that's exactly what I told her. She stopped flirting with me and moved on."

I was the one he'd *wanted*. Past tense. Just because we were talking again didn't mean he still had feelings for me. Did it? Besides, he'd kissed Josie *before* prom. Why hadn't he put the brakes on Josie back then?

"So why did you stand me up that night at The Bean Pit?" he asked. "You couldn't at least text me?"

"Didn't think you'd notice." I shrugged and gave him an apologetic look. "At the time, I figured you'd find Josie or someone else to entertain you," I mumbled.

I heard a faint buzzing and eyed my phone at the same time Wyatt checked his.

"It's Colin," he said, reading a text. "I left him without a ride home and he has a strict curfew. We should head back." He stood and led the way back to his car.

Wyatt navigated the streets, focusing on his task. I gazed out the window and watched the street lamps whiz by. At the stop sign before Alex's house, he glanced over at me with a tentative smile.

He wasn't mad I'd stood him up that night? My heart melted.

A few houses later, he killed the engine. Instead of getting out, he rotated in his seat. "I get why you stood me up that night. I just wish you'd talked to me about it."

And I wished I'd get that confession. Still, at least it seemed we were friends again. And I'd missed him. I forced a smile and exited the Camaro.

Several people stood on the lawn chatting. They turned their heads when we neared the front door. Probably wondering if Wyatt and I were an item again.

"You guys missed a great game of Truth or Dare," Tommy said, his arm draped around Alex's shoulders. "Colin had to streak down the block in his underwear."

"It was awesome." Alex's lips curved up. "I was wondering where you went off to," she told me.

"Just went out for coffee." I said, relieved I'd somehow avoided all the 'fun.' I hated that game. Someone always asked me about my first kiss and I hated the look in everyone's eyes when I had to spill my lack of experience. So I avoided it, hoping that if enough time passed, everyone would assume that I'd finally been kissed.

"Where'd you park?" Wyatt asked.

"At home," I said. Somehow, his hand had found its way to my lower back and a tingle ran up my spine. "Laynie picked me up."

"Maybe she won't mind if... if I drive you home."

I blinked, my reply sticking in my throat. Why would he drive me home? And why was his hand on my back? Was he interested again? Or still? Yes, I desperately wanted him to want me. Except what would ensure he wouldn't cheat again?

It may never work out with us, but I wasn't ready to say goodnight.

"That'd be great." My stomach flipped. "Uh... let me run in and tell Laynie. While I'm in there, I'll get Colin."

Inside, I found Laynie talking to a couple of friends from school. She spotted me, said something to them and dashed over to me.

"What happened?" she whispered. "You've been gone forever and I've been dying to know. Is he still here? Or did you scare him off?"

I couldn't stop the grin, happy just being near him again without either of us arguing. Besides, I hadn't given up that last bit of hope that maybe, just maybe, he'd say something to make me trust him again. "He's waiting for me outside to drive me home. Just wanted to let you know."

Laynie patted her heart and sighed. "So, what are you waiting for? Go." She turned me around and shoved me all the way to the front door.

"Just one problem. Would you drive Colin home, so I'll have more time with Wyatt?" I asked, facing her again.

She nodded. "Sure."

"Thanks." I threw her a smile over my shoulder, then hurried outside.

"Laynie says she'll drive Colin home," I said once I reached the bottom of the steps.

"Awesome," Wyatt answered, his face breaking into a grin.

Alex didn't budge from her cozy position, her back against Tommy with his arms overlapping her stomach. "I'll call you tomorrow," she said, a knowing gleam in her eye.

I bet she would. She'd want all the juicy details. Very likely, she was in for a huge disappointment. "Talk to you then," I said.

As Wyatt and I walked down the path toward the curb, my skin warmed from the gentle pressure of his fingertips on my lower back.

He opened the passenger side of his car, waited for me to get in, then closed the door.

I squeezed my eyes shut and took a deep breath, willing myself to relax. This was Wyatt, the guy who'd cheated on me. Didn't look like he was going to confess any time soon and, even if he did, he couldn't make it right. We'd never be more than friends. So I had nothing to be nervous about.

Except that I'd never stopped liking him. No matter what I'd witnessed and what I should feel, I still remembered our late-night phone conversations, the way he'd look at me with a smile in his eyes and the times he'd left chocolate in my locker.

But our relationship hadn't been real and would've never lasted without trust. I missed it anyway.

"You remember how to get to my house?" I asked.

"Of course." He started up the engine.

I swiveled to face him as he pulled the Camaro away from the curb. He had a gorgeous profile — a straight nose and a strong chin. Everything about him was perfect.

I was completely screwed.

When he rolled to a stop in front of my house, instead of letting the car idle and waiting for me to get out,

Wyatt killed the engine. I froze, unsure why he'd parked.

He pulled his keys from the ignition. "I'll walk you up."

"Thanks for the coffee and the ride," I said once I made it to the front door. I reached into my purse for my key, trying to ignore the urge to wrap my arms around him.

"Do you want to do something tomorrow? Maybe go to a movie?"

Yes. Definitely yes. Unfortunately, that wasn't going to happen. I couldn't stop myself from blurting, "Shall we meet at The Bean Pit so I can catch you kissing Josie again?"

"What?" Wyatt frowned, looking totally confused. "Why would you think I kissed her at The Bean Pit?"

"Oh, come on! Admit it." As the memory assaulted me yet again, I struggled to choke out the next words. "I saw you two that night."

Slowly, the creases between his brows disappeared as he got it. "You mean when she kissed me by my car?"

"Well, I don't know, Wyatt. How many kisses were there when you were about to be on a date with me?" I asked in a snarky tone. "I guess with all the making out, it's hard to remember which kiss I'm talking about."

"Hold up. I did *not* kiss her. She ambushed me. As soon as I got over the shock, I pushed her away."

"You expect me to buy that?" I jingled my keys and spun to face my door. "Oh, please."

"Is that why you stood me up? Because you thought I'd hooked up with Josie?" He nudged my shoulder until I was facing him again. His jaw tightened. "If you'd stayed, you would've seen for yourself what really happened. Or, if you'd talked to me about what you thought you saw, I could've defended myself."

"If you hadn't already had a problem telling her no, maybe I would have!"

He blew out a breath and squeezed his eyes shut. "I can see why you'd think that. But, Brittany, Josie's liked me since sixth grade. I've had lots of chances to kiss her, but I've never taken her up on it." His voice softened. "The Friday night before you stopped taking my calls, when you needed help proofreading the newspaper, where was I?"

I blinked. "With me."

"Where am I now?" he whispered, then waited a beat. "I *never* wanted Josie. Just *you*."

Facts didn't lie. If he had wanted to be with Josie, he would've been. The kiss really had been all one-sided and Wyatt was innocent. I'd dumped him for nothing. Oh, God, what an idiot I'd been. I lowered my gaze to blink away a tear. "I guess I jumped to conclusions. I'm sorry."

Wyatt stepped forward and reached up to move my hair off my shoulder. "I've missed you."

I gave him a watery smile. "I've missed you, too."

His hand found my back again and this time his other hand came around, encircling me. "What are you doing tomorrow?"

"Hanging out with you?" I felt my cheeks heat.

He flashed me a smile. "It's a date."

I'd screwed up big time, but he was willing to give us another chance. This time, I wouldn't blow it. Palms on his chest, I reached up and brushed my lips against his cheek. His hands tightened around my waist and he pulled me closer. His gaze dropped to my lips and I knew what was coming.

My first kiss. With Wyatt—the only guy I'd ever wanted.

I tilted my chin up, closed my eyes and a moment later his mouth touched mine. His lips moved softly, his warm breath whispering a silent promise.

Then, suddenly, a breeze brushed my lips and I opened my eyes.

Wow.

"Sorry. I've been wanting to do that all night," he said in a hoarse voice. "Longer actually. So when Alex told me she thought you might still like me, I —"

"She did *what*?" I felt my eyes bulge, but then it occurred to me that if she hadn't told him, Wyatt probably wouldn't have come to the party, much less followed me outside when I'd been leaving. My annoyance faded quickly. "So, if she hadn't said that, you wouldn't be talking to me right now?"

He shrugged. "Not talking to you was killing me. But I was afraid if I tried, you'd tell me to piss off."

"I hated not talking to you," I said. All the awkwardness slipped away as if we'd never been apart. I wound my arms around his neck and smiled. "Now, where were we?"

He grinned and kissed me again. This time, our tongues brushed and a shiver ran up my spine. I tilted my head to take the kiss deeper and he wrapped his arms tighter around me, pressing me closer. He tasted sweeter than my dreams. As our mouths melted together, my limbs turned to boneless mush and I held onto him for support.

The front door opened and he jumped back. From the doorway, my mom stared at Wyatt who stood rooted to the steps, wide-eyed.

"Hi, Wyatt. Nice to see you again." My mom's eyes darted from him to me. I blushed.

"Uh, h-hi, Mrs. H," Wyatt said. His cheeks turned pink.

"It's late, sweetheart. Come inside soon," she told me, then winked at me and closed the door.

"How embarrassing." I rested my forehead on his shoulder, figuring my face had to be flushed too.

"More so for me, I think. But at least it wasn't your dad." Wyatt gave a nervous laugh. "Hey, before I go, there's something I've been wanting to ask you..."

I looked at him curiously. "What's that?"

He shifted his weight to his other foot. "What are you doing for prom?"

If that was his way of asking me to be his date, he'd have to do better than that. "A little dancing, maybe drink some punch. You?"

He snorted. "No, I mean, would you... do you want to go with me?"

I d gotten my first kiss from my dream guy and he'd just asked me to prom—all in one night. Being singled out by my friends had been a great idea after all. I couldn't wait to reciprocate and team up with Alex to get Laynie a prom date. It was my duty, right? But at the moment, I was a little preoccupied.

Wyatt's face fell. "Or do you already have a date?"

I laid my palms on either side of his face. "I do now. You're the only one I want." And I kissed him again.

The End

Single-minded

Veronica Blade

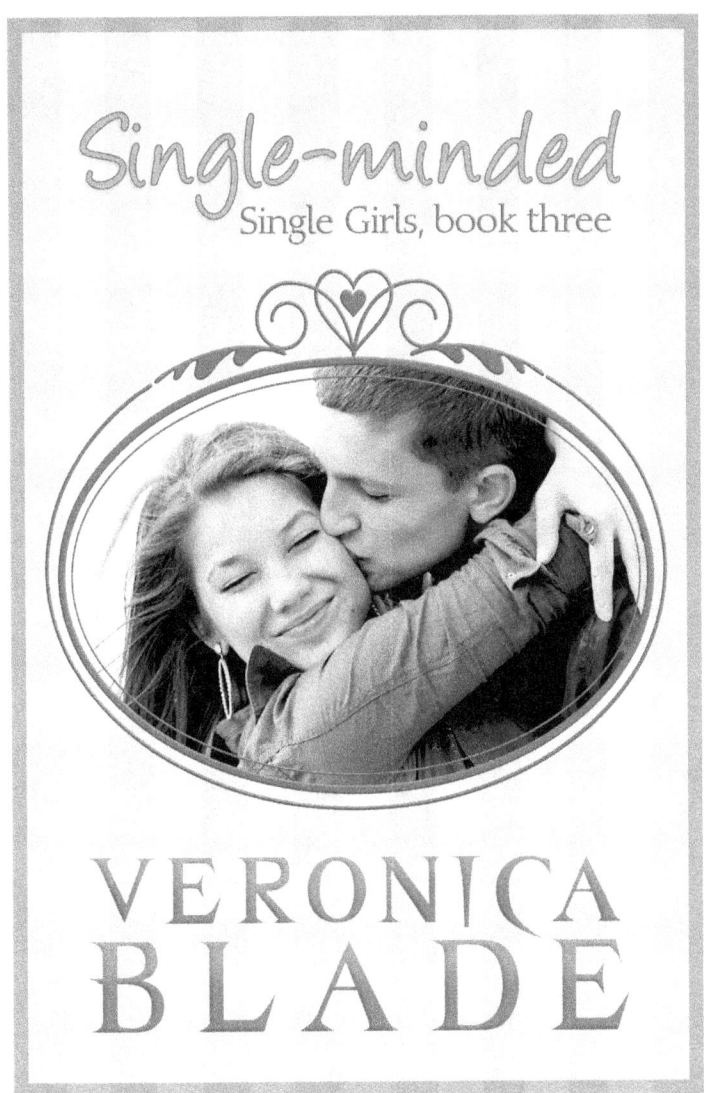

Chapter One

Wyatt stopped at a red light as I pressed the end button and shoved my cell back in my purse — just in time to see him lean over and kiss Brittany in the passenger seat.

In less than a block, I'd be home and no longer subject to my friends' PDA. My house loomed ahead with its white clapboard and red trimmed windows. And right out front sat a red Porsche, which meant my older brother's best friend was over. Even if he was with his bimbo-of-the-week, being home was still a better option than watching my friend make out with her new boyfriend.

She withdrew her hand from Wyatt's and twisted around in the front to face me. Like magnets, their hands found each other again. A pang of jealousy hit me. I'd been wanting a boyfriend for so long, yet I was the one going to prom alone.

"So what did your dad say?" she asked.

We rolled to a stop in front of my house and I leaned forward, sticking my head between her seat and Wyatt's. "He says it has a cracked block. Whatever that means. It'll be in the shop at least a week."

After two days without a car, I already felt like a burden to my friends. I sighed at the thought of mooching rides all next week too.

"Don't stress over it." Brittany gave me a reassuring smile, then climbed out and pulled her seat forward, so I could squeeze out. "Between the four of us, we'll get you to school every day."

Maybe I'd be better off hitching a ride from one of my parents. Brittany and Alex plus their boyfriends made me the obvious odd girl out. It was worse when we watched a movie together and they were doing *other things* and not looking at the screen at all.

Seeing my two best friends so happy didn't make me regret my part in getting them boyfriends. But even though I knew they weren't ignoring me intentionally, I hated feeling like an outsider. Staying home and watching TV or diving into a good book seemed like way more fun than being reminded that I didn't have what I wanted so badly — a real boyfriend.

If I had Alex's long, dark brown hair, olive skin and black, exotic eyes or Brittany's big boobs, blond hair or brains, maybe I wouldn't be boyfriendless. Instead, I got cursed with hair everyone referred to as red — though it was more like a burnt orange — and paste-like skin. And if I didn't use enough product, my hair frizzed and came out looking like tumbleweeds. Don't even get me started on the splotchy freckles dotting my face.

"Thanks." I forced a smile and stepped onto the curb. "Let's play each day by ear. Sometimes my mom's good for a ride. Or maybe my parents will suddenly feel generous and buy me a new car," I said hopefully.

If only they could buy me a prom date as easily. Actually, they could. But if I were desperate enough to hire an escort, I might as well consider my other options—Luke or Aiden. They'd both asked me to prom, which was sweet. But I wasn't interested in either of them, not as a boyfriend. It didn't feel right to lead them on. Plus, there was the distinct possibility that they'd only asked me because no other girls were available. That wasn't good enough for me.

"Maybe they'll get you a convertible and we can all drive with *you*." Brittany grinned.

And embrace being the fifth wheel? No way. "Thanks so much for the ride. I'll call you later." I smiled again and headed across the lawn to my house. The TV blared as I turned the doorknob. "Hey, Josh."

My big brother's best friend muted the TV and looked up from the couch, giving me a subtle nod. "Hey, Laynie."

He looked as delish as always. But since he usually treated me like his little sister, I tried to act accordingly and not think about how hot he was. With the TV silenced, I noticed the rest of the house was completely quiet too.

"Where is everyone?" I asked, dropping my backpack near the dining room table.

"Your parents said something about getting an early start on date night."

Right. My dad told me that five minutes ago. "And Chris?" I asked.

"At the store."

"Why aren't you with him?" Not that I should complain about being with Josh when it was clearly the highlight of my depressing day. "Instead, you're all alone in someone else's house? A bit creepy, don't you think?"

Josh was far from creepy — which is why I felt compelled to give him a hard time. It kept me from letting on what a mammoth crush I had for him. I grabbed my calculus book from my backpack, laid it in front of me on the dining room table and took a seat.

"I knew you'd be home soon." Josh tossed the remote on the couch and stood, lifting one brown brow. "Don't act like it's weird to see me here."

It would be weirder *not* to see him at my house every day with Chris. I'd met his parents a few times, just like my mom had. To say they were crappy parents would be grossly exaggerating their parental skills. Which is why my mom gave Josh a standing invitation to dinner — one that he used frequently.

Josh vacated the living room and leaned against the doorway that lead to the kitchen. "It's not like we've never hung out before."

"When we were *kids*." I shot him a look of annoyance.

"So we're not friends anymore?" He stalked over to me. "Too mature for that now?"

I blinked. More like *Josh* was too mature for *me*. Since he and my brother had started college last fall, I saw a lot less of them. I'd gotten more of Josh's attention the last few minutes than I had in months. Why was he was still talking to me? It wasn't exactly a hardship, but I didn't want him to know that.

"Of course not." Opening the book, I focused on my assignment.

"Good." Reaching forward, he touched my hair. "You should let it go curly more often. I like it this way."

My blood hummed and my heart pumped faster. Talking to me in that low, sexy voice *and* touching my hair? "Seriously?"

Tempted as I was to wear it curly every day just to please him, I wouldn't allow myself to hope his sudden attention meant anything. Renewing my ancient crush on him would only lead to revisiting an old heartache. I'd never go there again. Too painful.

Josh wasn't a douche like some guys, but no girl had been able to hold his attention for long—he went through girls like he went through food. And Josh could eat a lot.

Chris's little sister would never be on Josh's menu. Any girl he'd ever brought over had looked like they should be posing on the hood of a sports car wearing next to nothing. I was more the spectator type. Not exciting enough for a guy like Josh.

I jerked a shoulder to dodge his hand, trying to ignore the fluttering in my stomach. "Eew. The only thing worse than red hair is *curly* red hair."

"Really?" He tilted his head, looking perplexed. "I always liked it."

"Where's Terese?" I asked, unable to stop myself.

He snorted. "We broke up weeks ago."

"Oh." I wished him being single didn't make my heart pump harder. "Dumped her, huh?"

"Why do you always assume I'm the dumper and not the dumpee?" He folded his arms over his chest and straightened his spine.

Obviously, I wasn't going to get any homework done with him around, which was fine, because he was far more interesting. I shoved the calculus book aside, rose and rested a hip against the table. "So you're saying she dumped you?"

"No." He gave me a lopsided smile. "I broke up with her."

Of course. A girl would be a total idiot to dump him. And judging by Josh's twitching mouth, I guessed he was enjoying messing with me. "So who are you dating now?" I asked, trying not to sound like I cared.

"Who says I'm dating anyone at all?"

I stared at him blankly. As long as I could remember, Josh always had a girl in his life. When I was seven, and he and Chris were eight, he'd hold hands with Dia Williams behind the school. Then it was Kristin, then April. The list went on.

Josh wasn't as pretty as Alex's boyfriend Tommy or Brittany's boyfriend Wyatt. His nose was almost too big, but his cheekbones and strong chin balanced it out. It didn't hurt that he was tall with wide shoulders and thick, brown hair. And there was something else that made him just as hot as Tommy or Wyatt. Maybe it was the confidence he oozed or his sense of humor.

He'd been like a brother to me practically my entire life — except in my fantasies when he'd kissed me. But I tried to avoid those kinds of thoughts or analyzing why girls were drawn to him. Why *I* was drawn to him.

To avoid falling into another one of his verbal traps, I passed him and made my way to the fridge.

"Wow, you just don't keep up on my love life at all, do you?" He'd followed me into the kitchen and leaned against the counter, smirking.

I planted my hands on my hips and glared at him. "Are you going to answer every question with a question? Why are you being so weird? Do you have a girlfriend or not?"

One side of his mouth curled up. "Why do you want to know?"

I'd walked right into that one. I found the apple juice, then closed the door and returned his smirk. "Actually, I don't. Besides, keeping up with the girls in your life would be a full-time job."

"Not these days." Josh's expression grew serious, then he frowned and reached into his pocket. He pulled out his cell and looked at the flashing screen. With a flick of his thumb, he rejected the call and set his phone on the counter.

Glancing down, I read *Missed call from Kendra* as it flashed. Didn't look to me like anything had changed. I motioned him aside and he scooted along the counter.

I grabbed a glass near his head. "College girls aren't as exciting as you thought they'd be?" I asked.

"Maybe I'm looking for something more." He lifted a shoulder.

"So, what, you're into older women now or something?" I asked, trying not to imagine him with *any* girl much less someone far more sophisticated than me.

"No, I mean I want a real relationship."

His phone dinged and I sneaked a peek. A text from Michelle. Well, he may say he wants a real relationship, but with all the girls calling and texting him, I had my doubts that he could pick one and stay for very long.

"You'd be satisfied with one person when every girl you meet is falling all over you?" I poured the juice into the glass.

"Not *every* girl, Laynie," he said, pointedly. "*You've* never been into me."

Little did he know — and hopefully he never would.

Josh was standing so close I could smell him. And he smelled *good*, like rain and worn leather. I drew in a long breath and his scent rushed through me and warmed my insides.

"Oh, please. As if I'm your type," I said, sipping from my glass and trying to ignore the flush creeping up my neck.

He stared at me intently.

"Sorry to hear you're having dating issues. If you

need a girl's viewpoint, maybe I can help. So what's the problem?"

He stepped a foot or two away and picked up a trivet. Setting it back down, he shoved a hand in his pocket. "I'm tired of random dating."

"Yeah, I guess having your pick of girls gets pretty old." I snorted, then sipped from the glass again.

His gaze didn't waver as one long stride put him directly in front of me. "But I don't want them."

His phone vibrated on the counter behind him. Another girl, no doubt.

I couldn't read Josh's expression, but if I were a fly on the wall watching this scene play out, I'd guess Josh was trying to hook up with me. But that was impossible, since Josh didn't feel that way — not about *me*.

If he really was interested, I'd put money on his reason being that I was one of the few girls who didn't try to hook up with him. That wasn't a good enough reason for me to risk getting dumped.

Or maybe he wasn't coming onto me at all… I could feel my eyebrows straining to meet in the middle as I struggled to figure out what he was up to. "Is something wrong? You're acting freaky."

"You're not getting it." He studied me. "I don't want to date other girls."

I was more confused than ever. "You're switching teams?"

"No." Josh moved closer, reached a hand out to take my glass, then he set it on the counter. Bringing both of his hands up to cup my neck, he bent toward me. "Just narrowing my focus."

My eyes bulged and I froze, incapable of stopping what I knew was about to happen.

Not that I *wanted* to stop it.

Chapter Two

I didn't resist as Josh's mouth covered mine, gently teasing my lips apart. Josh, who used to beat me in *Go Fish* was *kissing* me. The same Josh I'd crushed on *forever.* Kissing *me.* I couldn't think, much less question why, because all activity in my brain ceased when I opened wider for him and his tongue tangled with mine.

It had been a while since I'd been kissed. Even longer since I'd been kissed *right.* Josh was definitely doing it right.

My fingers dug into his waist and I pressed against him. Tingles raced from my chest all the way to my toes. Suddenly, I couldn't breathe. And I didn't care if I ever breathed again, so long as Josh kept kissing me.

Then he straightened, our mouths separating just a fraction of an inch, my breath coming in short, quick gasps. I stared up at him, unable to move or look away.

If I were smart, I would've used that moment to escape so I didn't get in any deeper. I mean, talk about setting myself up for heartbreak.

The gentle pressure of his palms at the side of my face coaxed me backward and a moment later, I was against the stove.

"What are we doing?" I asked.

"Playing *Go Fish*. No clear winner yet," he whispered, just before he lowered his mouth to mine again. This time, his teeth nibbled my bottom lip until I ached for more.

My pulse raced and my lungs worked faster as if I were oxygen deprived. His thumb at my jaw parted my lips and he dove again. Heat burned through my veins.

The front door slammed. I sidestepped and leaped away from Josh. Grabbing my glass of juice, I attempted to act casual. I knew my brother would find us any second and I hoped he wouldn't see me blushing. I didn't want to look guilty—like I'd just been kissing his best friend.

"Josh? Laynie? Where are you guys?" he called from the living room.

Josh cleared his throat. "In the kitchen." He was still watching me, his eyes dark and his lids heavy.

Chris appeared a moment later, smiling and glancing from me to Josh. "What's going on?" he asked, setting a brown paper bag on the counter.

Josh's cell phone rattled against the kitchen counter. I mentally palmed my forehead. What was I thinking to believe, even for a moment, that a kiss would mean anything to Josh? I couldn't compete against all the hot girls I'd seen him with or the girls calling and texting, much less hold his attention longer than they did.

"Why would you think something's going on?" I snapped.

Chris raised his hands high. "Whoa. Just curious what you guys were up to while I was gone."

Ever cool, Josh punched Chris in the shoulder. "Nothing. Just waiting for you."

No, nothing at all. Certainly not kissing his best friend's little sister. No, that would be forbidden territory.

I had to get out of there.

"Stopped to get gas and ran into Mr. Chandler. Got a lecture on safe sex when he caught me looking at the porn magazines. Not like I could get to them from the other side of the counter. What a douche. Did I miss anything?"

Yep. Chris had missed plenty. But the last thing I wanted to do was talk to my brother about his best friend... who'd very likely been acting on impulse and probably already regretted kissing me. Whatever love crisis he was going through, I refused to be his guinea pig or a band-aid for his problem. "I think I'll do my homework upstairs. See you guys later."

Avoiding eye contact with both of them, I set my glass on the counter, snatched my books off the dining room table, then rocketed up the stairs to my room.

When dinnertime rolled around, their voices still wafted up the stairs. Facing my brother and wondering if he knew what had happened didn't seem appealing. The prospect of seeing regret in Josh's eyes for kissing me didn't exactly seem like a thrill ride either. Especially since my reaction to his kiss had been so enthusiastic. Talk about giving it all away.

So I skipped dinner in favor of solitude and a chocolate bunny left over from Easter.

~~~

The next morning, I staggered into my bathroom to wash up. My thoughts drifted to Josh—again. As if they'd ever been off him since *the kiss*. I'd tossed and turned and awakened too many times to count and each time I'd thought of him. That led to contemplating his motives for kissing me like *that*. Me! Then I'd be wide awake again.

Splashing cold water on my face, I hoped my eyelids didn't try to catch up on sleep by closing during English Lit. We had a test today. Even if I managed to stay awake, I doubted concentration would come easy.

I shoved my toothbrush around in my mouth, debating whether Josh genuinely liked me or if the kiss had been a whim. He could have anyone he wanted. Why bother with a high-schooler when he could go out with someone more experienced?

After rinsing the toothpaste from my mouth, I headed for the stairs.

Josh knew I was a settle-down kind of girl, looking for *the guy*. He wouldn't risk his friendship with my brother just to toy with me. The small bit of hope that had sparked when he'd kissed me ignited in my chest again. But then.... why hadn't he said goodbye when he'd left our house? Or at least texted me?

Or maybe he *would* toy with me. We hadn't been close in years, so how well did I really know him anymore? He was only nineteen and no way would he want to tie himself down to one girl. He couldn't. No matter what he said. Right? At that thought, my limbs felt sluggish as I descended the stairs.

So if he wasn't truly interested in a future with me, what was he doing? Experimenting to see what it felt like to date a good girl? See if he still had the magic touch? Or maybe he'd had a dry spell and now even his best friend's little sister was starting to look pretty good.

I paused at the first landing, trying to push away thoughts of Josh. Unless I asked him what was up, I'd never know. But I couldn't risk him saying to my face that he'd only forgotten himself for a moment. No way.

I sucked in a lungful of air and the scent of brewing coffee hit me. Hm... Mom and Dad would already be halfway to work by now, and they rarely made coffee in the mornings anyway. Chris could barely get up in time to get himself ready, much less make coffee.

Josh usually stayed over when his dad was on a drinking binge — which was once or twice a week. Looked like last night had been one of those nights.

If I wanted to avoid having my heart crushed, I had to avoid him. Unfortunately, Josh would spot me from the kitchen as soon as I hit the bottom of the stairs. My stomach tightened. I didn't want to be rude by getting caught trying to escape, which meant that speaking to him was inevitable.

I paused at the bottom step. Josh's short brown hair stuck out in every direction and his t-shirt sported a hole big enough for a fist to pass through. Yet he still looked scrumptious. Warm tingles danced in my belly as I remembered yesterday's kiss.

Until I could sort out my feelings — and his intentions — I needed to steer clear of him. Which meant not encouraging him or letting on how much he affected me. If my hunch was right and he didn't have strong feelings for me, there was no point in him feeling guilty for last night's kiss. That would only make things more awkward.

I made my way to the kitchen. Josh stopped stirring the eggs in the pan, then his eyes locked on mine. "Good morning," he said, a smile forming on his lips. "Hungry?"

"Starved," I answered, rounding the counter to stand behind him.

"Promised these to Josh, but I'll make yours next."

"Thanks." I gave him a shy smile, then dived for the coffee on the opposite counter.

He eyed me as I reached into the cupboard for a mug. "Didn't see your car outside," he said. "Thought maybe you'd left early."

"It's in the shop." I kept my voice neutral, like nothing had happened between us. Except that pretending was one thing — forgetting a kiss like that would be much more difficult.

"I have time before my first class to give you a ride to school."

I opened the fridge to get cream for my coffee. When I felt his gaze on my back, I glanced over my shoulder. "Thanks, but Alex is picking me up."

Chris passed through the kitchen doorway, snorted, then gave Josh a friendly punch in the arm. "Why make Alex drive out of her way when Bozo here can drive you? It'll give him a chance to earn his keep."

My brother had the worst timing ever. If I refused Josh's offer now, Chris might think something was up... he might find out Josh and I had kissed. Awkward. Worse, I could hurt Josh's feelings if he thought I didn't want to be around him. Kiss or no kiss, he was still a friend.

"Okay, sure." I took a sip from the mug. "I'll text Alex. Will you be ready to leave in twenty minutes?" I risked a glance at him.

"No problem." Josh turned off the burner and moved the pan, then turned to face me again.

"Thanks," I said, shifting my weight to my other leg.

"So, Layn, any luck getting a prom date?" my incredibly tactless brother asked as he opened the fridge.

My cheeks heated and I mumbled through clenched teeth, "Uh, no."

"Nobody's asked you?" Josh studied me.

"Yeah, but nobody I'd want to go with. I'd rather go alone." I added a little more cream to my coffee, just for something to do.

"Nice pajamas," Josh said.

Masochist that I am, I returned my attention to him.

His gaze traveled up my bare legs, to my flannel boxer-like shorts, then landed on my thin tank top. When he met my eyes again, his own darkened. He had that same look he'd given me yesterday, just before he'd kissed me. My heart skipped a beat.

Wait. Where was Chris? Apparently, he'd grown bored of my prom drama and vanished. If I didn't move soon, Josh would think I was waiting for a repeat performance of last night. I turned, grabbed the mug and bailed, secretly wishing he would stop me.

My parents met in high school, got married right away and had been together ever since. They still looked at each other with the same adoring eyes and often exchanged meaningful smiles. Like they were so in love, neither could imagine their lives without the other.

Call me a romantic, but I wanted what they had. It's not like I wanted to get married. Not right now anyway. But casual dating held no interest for me. Why waste time dating a bunch of duds? Why settle for less than what I really wanted?

Twenty minutes later, dressed with more care than usual, I descended the steps again. I wasn't petite and incredibly fit like Alex or blond and brainy like Brittany. But I'd danced since I was nine and had plenty of toned curves. The camisole and short black skirt would ensure Josh saw enough of them. And I wore my hair curly... because he'd said he liked it. And because if Josh wasn't interested in me as more than a friend, he needed to know what he was missing.

Josh whistled, then said, "You look nice."

Under normal circumstances, I'd tease him for getting his perv on. Now, I wasn't sure how to act. "Thanks." I listened for other sounds in the house, but didn't hear anything. "Chris left?"

"Yeah. He said goodbye, but I guess you didn't hear." He reached into his pocket and pulled out his keys. "Ready to go?"

I nodded and followed him out the door, locking up behind me. When I turned, he'd already reached his car and opened the passenger side door. He had his mom's red Porsche today. I theorized that his parents overcompensated for their neglect by giving him things or letting him borrow theirs. Today, I certainly wasn't going to complain.

The engine roared and he put the car into drive. "I have a light class schedule today. I'll pick you up after school."

"You don't have to. Really. I can get a ride." Josh plus Porsche beat being a third or fifth wheel any day. But not today, not so soon after that kiss.

Josh chuckled and stopped at a red light. "Why are you being difficult? I've given you rides before."

Because your cell phone is probably vibrating as we speak and it's only a matter of time before you take a call from some other girl.

"I don't want you going out of your way." I pivoted in my seat so I couldn't see him at all.

"It's no bother, since I'm going to your house later anyway."

"But my school isn't on your way," I pointed out, my gaze steady on the passing buildings.

"Getting rides from me never bothered you before."

"You never kissed me before," I blurted out. Damn. Now I couldn't pretend it never happened. I shifted in my seat to face him.

"True." He glanced over his shoulder, changed lanes and pulled over. Killing the engine, he turned toward me. "Do you have something you want to say about that?" he asked softly.

Yes, I did. But I didn't want to accuse him of toying with me. And if he really was messing with me, I didn't want him to think I cared. I fidgeted and gazed out the window on my side, so all he saw was my hair.

"Just say what's on your mind, Layn."

"Why did you kiss me?" I faced him again to gauge his reaction.

"Maybe..." His gaze darted away as his fingertips tapped the steering wheel. "Maybe it just took me a while to work up the nerve."

To work up the nerve to kiss his best friend's totally unglamorous, redheaded little sister? My lips parted and I just stared at him. There was always a catch when something was too good to be true. On the other hand, it was hard to believe that he would admit to working up the nerve if he didn't care, at least a little.

"You okay?" Josh asked, his gaze pausing briefly on dashboard clock. "Damn. You're going to be late for school."

Josh started up the car again and merged with traffic. He didn't say anything else and my brain was too scattered. He'd been wanting to kiss me and he did. But where did that leave us? Did he want to do it again or were we back to being friends?

When he pulled up to the curb, he said, "I'll be here after school to take you home."

Too stunned to argue, I nodded and made my escape without even thanking him for the ride.

Chapter Three

"Laynie, is something wrong?" Alex asked me.

I glanced up from my lunch tray. "No, why?"

She eyed my pizza. "If that were a frog, you'd totally get an A in biology."

I lowered my gaze again. She was right. The cheese was sectioned off and the pepperonis organized into piles. I hadn't even been aware I'd been playing with my food.

"You seem really distracted," Brittany weighed in.

My eyes met Alex's again, then Brittany's and finally to Tommy and Wyatt — who were also staring at me. Even if I could dissect my feelings, like I did my lunch, I certainly wouldn't talk about it in front of Tommy or Wyatt. And who knew when I'd have any alone time with the girls again?

"No big deal. I'm just worried about Josh."

"Is his dad on another drinking binge?" Brittany asked.

"He looked okay when I saw him pulling out of the parking lot this morning," Wyatt chimed in.

"Yeah, I guess he's fine," I muttered. The warning bell rang and I dumped my tray, then headed for the restroom. Brittany and Alex followed.

"So what's really wrong?" Brittany asked.

I groaned, knowing we didn't have time for a full debrief on everything that had happened.

"And don't give us that crap about being worried about Josh." Alex gave me a warning look.

I ducked low and checked the stalls to make sure we were alone. "Josh kissed me yesterday."

Brittany tilted her head, a blank look on her face. "Josh who?"

"Josh, the permanent fixture at my house," I said.

"Oh." Alex's mouth curved up. "And this is a bad thing?"

"I'm going with no," Brittany added. "Nothing's bad with a guy that hot."

"Yeah, he's hot, but that's the problem. He's always with some gorgeous girl, so what would he want with me?"

Brittany waved a hand in front of me. "Wait. You're going too fast. Was there, like, tongue and everything?"

My stomach flipped as I recalled his mouth on mine. "Oh, yeah."

"You obviously like him." Alex nudged my rib with her elbow. "I'm sorry, but I don't see a problem."

I batted her elbow away. "Yeah, I've crushed on him forever, but I can't picture him settling for just one girl, much less me." I shook my head. "There's no happy ending for me, not with Josh."

"You act like you're a leper and that's ridiculous." Alex rolled her eyes. "You're just as pretty as any girl I've seen him with. Different type, but maybe that's what he wants."

"Exactly. He kissed you—that's *huge*." Brittany grasped my shoulders. "Do you realize how many girls would die to be you right now?"

Were my friends not listening to me? "It's obviously nothing to him. I was handy, just another girl to kiss, you know?"

"Then he spent the night and gave you a ride to school. It has to mean something." Alex bumped my elbow again.

They were naïve to assume that Josh kissing me automatically meant he was serious about me. Whatever. "We'd better go or we're going to be late for class."

They sighed in unison, but I wasn't stupid enough to think that meant they were giving up.

~~~

After last class, just inside the big double doors that led to the parking lot, I spotted Alex and Brittany approaching.

Brittany sidled up to me, eyes wide. "I still can't get over Josh kissing you."

Alex huddled with us. "He's a great guy and he's hot. I say go for it."

Wow, they hadn't heard a thing I'd said and they obviously didn't know Josh at all. "What?"

"Didn't you like the kiss?" Brittany asked.

"Or did he screw it up?" Alex asked. "He didn't bathe you in saliva, did he?"

I held up my hands to stop the barrage of questions. "First, he's *Josh*. I've known him most of my life."

Brittany and Alex exchanged glances. "And?" they asked in unison.

I released my breath in a whoosh. "And it was *amazing*."

My friends beamed. "So go get him," Alex said.

"He's not into me." I rubbed my temple. Pursuing Josh meant rejection. The concept of that kind of epic disaster made my head pound.

Brittany scoffed. "Not possible."

"Yeah." Alex swiped my shoulder. "Quit being a girl. If he didn't like you that way, he wouldn't have kissed you."

Brittany nodded decisively. "I concur."

"You shouldn't keep him waiting." Alex turned me around by my shoulders and gently shoved me out the door.

"Call us later with all the juicy details. 'Bye now," Brittany sang with a grin.

I stumbled outside and the bright sunlight scorched my eyes. Using my hand as a shield, I scanned the lot for Josh. Spotting his red Porsche in the corner toward the back, I took a deep breath to calm the butterflies in my stomach as I started toward it. Josh was leaning against the passenger side, his ankles crossed.

Could the kiss have meant something to him, like Brittany and Alex believed? Or had he only been satisfying a longtime curiosity?

He grinned and opened the car door. "Your chariot, milady."

I smiled back, despite the cheesy words. He was so damned cute. His pocket dinged and he reached in to retrieve his phone.

Another girl, no doubt. But why did his jaw go slack when he read the text? "What's wrong?" I asked.

He blinked, then focused on me. "You can read it yourself, but let's get on the road first."

I climbed into the passenger seat as he rounded the hood. Once he'd driven through the school gates and was cruising down the street, he handed me his cell. The last text had been from Alex. As I read it, the air froze in my lungs.

She likes u. Hurt her & I'll hurt u :-)

Alex had just outed me. Payback was a bitch. And, oh, God, Josh was wearing his serious face. Obviously, because he didn't like me in that way. I stifled a sob and handed Josh his phone, then turned to stare out the window, too mortified to speak. Hoping the heat in my cheeks would cool, I straightened in my seat as I caught a glimpse of a passing street sign. This wasn't the way to my house. "Where are we going?"

"Somewhere private, so we can talk."

I gulped at his grave tone. "Where?"

"The beach. It's a weekday, so it won't be crowded." He spared me a quick glance before returning his attention to the road.

He'd better not be taking us all the way to the beach just to tell me that the kiss had been a mistake and meant nothing. How would I endure the drive back with him after that? I became queasy, my hands trembling and my throat stinging.

The ocean reflected the afternoon sun and the seagulls floated in the sky. Pedestrians, clad in shorts and sandals, crossed the street ahead. As the Porsche slowed, I rolled down the window to inhale the smell of sand and sea.

After a couple more blocks, Josh parked. I got out and waited for him. Waves crashed against the sand and a breeze lifted my hair.

"Laynie."

I whirled around.

"Shoes." He pointed at my feet and flashed me a grin. "Off."

He'd already removed his sneakers and rolled up his jeans. I nodded and obeyed, then he stowed them in the car and jerked his head toward the foaming water. "Let's walk," he said.

I took a deep breath, chastising myself for being happy just to be near him. He was being awfully sweet. For now. Until he broke my heart, that is. And my heart *would* break, because even though I tried to prepare myself for the big letdown, I couldn't help but hope that the kiss and the walk on the beach meant something to him. That maybe it meant as much to him as it did to me.

Wet sand squeezed between my toes just inches from the white foam nearly hitting our feet. If Josh didn't break the silence soon, I might start screaming and fling myself into the ocean.

"I'm sorry I ambushed you like that last night," Josh said as he continued walking. "It wasn't planned."

Oh, God. Here comes the axe.

"Why does Alex think you like me?" He peered over at me for a moment, then returned his focus ahead.

I unconsciously sucked in air again, then stopped. If we were going to have this conversation, I wanted his full attention. He stopped too. "Same reason she thinks *you* like *me*?" I guessed.

One side of his mouth lifted, forming a mischievous smile. "Has she been talking to your brother?"

"Is that what Chris would tell her?" I held my breath.

Josh's smiled disappeared as he shook his head. "No."

It felt as though a hundred needles pierced my chest at once. Of course Josh didn't *like* me. How silly I'd been to entertain the possibility that he could leave the realm of *brotherly* love for *me*.

Josh's eyes remained steady on mine. "Chris would say..."

"What?" Not that I wanted to know any more if I'd already lost him.

"... that I'm in love with you."

I gasped and my entire body tensed. "What?"

His gaze dropped to my mouth and he took a step closer, whispering, "I love you, Laynie."

My mind reeled. Accepting the possibility that he might actually like me as more than just a friend was challenging enough without fast-forwarding it to *love*. "Since when? I mean, I never even knew you liked me," I said. "This is… this is a lot to take in. Too fast."

"Not for me. I realized I loved you three years ago. But you always treated me like your brother, so I never did anything about it. But after yesterday, I'm hoping you see me differently."

I swallowed. All this time, he'd wanted me? "You sure? Because you've dated every other girl *but* me."

"That's why they didn't last. None of them were you."

I blinked. "But when you can have someone totally gorgeous like Terese, why would you want someone plain like me? It doesn't make any sense."

He shook his head. "You're just as beautiful. More so, even. And you're easier to be around. More fun."

My eyebrows shot up in alarm. I would've preferred words like irresistible, sexy or charming. *Fun* made me feel like a gal-pal. I grimaced. "Fun, huh?"

"We laugh together. It's why being with you never gets old. Besides, you let me win in Go Fish." He grinned.

"*Let* you? You're a card shark." I returned his smile. He was adorable and it felt like I was about to have it all. But there was always a catch, wasn't there? Could I be *that* lucky? Probably not, especially when girls were constantly calling him. It was only a matter of time before he talked to one of them. "Last night, we were in the kitchen maybe ten minutes and you got three calls.

That's an average of every three minutes. You're not ready to give them up."

Josh retrieved his phone from his pocket, threw his arm back and pitched his phone into the ocean. "When I get a new one, it'll have a different number." Then he moved until he was inches away from me, his smile crinkling the corners of his eyes. "So what do you think? You want to give it a shot?"

A new wave of white foam reached us, covering our feet, then slowly receding.

"Love is a big word." I looked away. Josh had been my fantasy guy for as long as I could remember, but was it *real* love that I felt for him? "Maybe you should give this more thought and make sure you're ready for a long-term relationship. You know I don't take dating lightly."

"Of course I know that." Somehow, we were almost touching now. "I want what you want. If you want it with me, I mean."

More than anything, I wanted to believe he cared deeply for me. Judging by his track record with girls though, I didn't think his feelings would last. I bit my bottom lip as I shifted and angled myself to put a little distance between us. It was easier to focus when he wasn't right up on me.

"You think I'd risk our friendship and your big brother's wrath if I didn't mean it?" he asked.

"No, of course not. I'm just trying to wrap my head around all this. I totally thought you drove me out here to blow me off. I'm happy to be wrong, believe me, but…"

"Laynie, just because I said I loved you doesn't mean you have to say it back. There's no pressure here."

I faced him again, my breath catching. Because I *did* want to say it back. Being with Josh felt so right, so comfortable. "Other than being fun, why choose *me*?" I asked.

He reached out and took my hand, pulling me closer until our lips were inches apart. "Because you see good in everyone, for starters. You're loyal and generous. Because you're smarter than me, but you never act like it. And anytime I picture myself years in the future, you're always there." He paused and searched my face, then lowered his voice. "And because you smell good."

I swallowed.

He interlaced his fingers with mine, his gaze unwavering. "Be honest, did you like kissing me yesterday?"

I nodded.

He smiled, a look of relief crossing his face. "And if I asked you to a movie Friday night, you might say yes?"

I nodded again, smiling.

"And you'd entertain the possibility of letting me escort you to prom?"

"I suppose so." I bit my bottom lip to hold back a grin.

"Then that's a better start than most couples have."

Josh was right. I couldn't force our future. But Josh would *try* and that's all anyone could hope for.

Thinking he might kiss me, I didn't look away. But the kiss didn't come. I gave him a mischievous smile and asked, "So are you going to kiss me again or what?"

"Thought you'd never ask." He laughed, but still didn't move. Instead, he reached out to touch my face. I covered his hand with mine and turned to kiss his palm. He pulled me against him, nuzzling his face in my hair.

"You're only saying all this because you're afraid Alex is going to kick your ass," I said, my words muffled by his shirt.

"Alex *is* terrifying." He chuckled, then drew back, his smile fading. He held my face with both hands and gazed into my eyes. "But not as terrifying as being without you."

"Then it's a good thing I'm not going anywhere." I slid my arms around his neck and pulled him to me.

The End

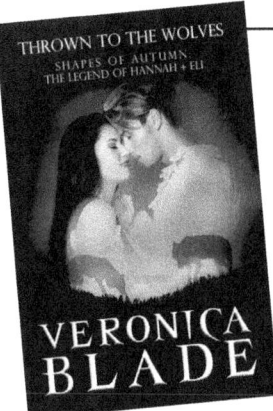

Free e-Book Offer

For a limited time, *Thrown To The Wolves: The Legend of Hannah & Eli (Shapes of Autumn Prequel)* is available for free from my website.

Find out more at VeronicaBlade.com

More Titles by Veronica Blade

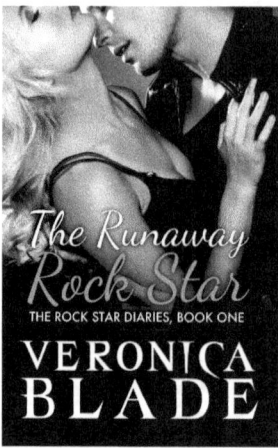

An infamous bad-boy rocker falls for a small-town girl who has no idea who he is. Considering his reputation, that's probably a good thing.

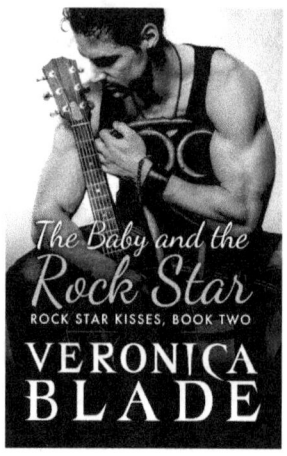

He's working hard to get his life back on track after three years of alcohol-induced oblivion. She can't forget their one wild night together—that he doesn't remember.

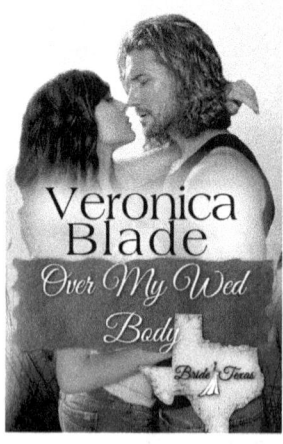

When Hunter realizes he botched the annulment of his marriage to his longtime friend, he must decide if she and their marriage are worth fighting for.

When good-girl Maddie switches places with her famous bad-girl twin Jackie, she has some pretty high stilettos to fill.

SHAPES OF AUTUMN SERIES

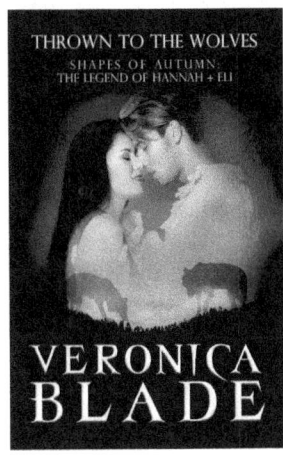

Thrown to the Wolves: The Legend of Hannah & Eli (prequel)

My Wolf's Bane (book one)

Wolves at the Door (book two)

Dead Wolf Walking (book three)

The Dark Wolf (book four)

Lord of the Wolves (book five)

Different species. Mortal enemies. It'll never work, but they'll die trying.

Should a woman who's unable to forget her first love give "happily ever after" one more try?

A Cinderella who spends her nights as a wolf. A prince with a taste for blood.

SOMETHING WITCHY SERIES

A newbie witch enlists help from the scrumptious school bad-boy to make her life and death choice between two battling covens.

The witch queen must make the impossible choice between abandoning the throne and her people, or spending eternity without the man she loves.

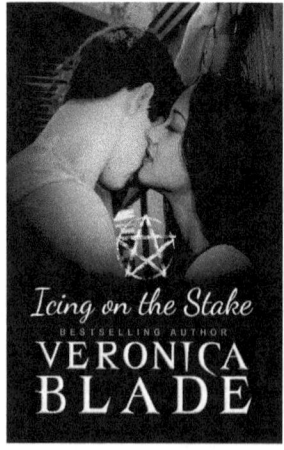

Sofia lays her hard-won anonymity on the line by saving the most popular boy in school. Worse, she's been exposed to the vampire hunters who attacked him.

)

For updates on releases,

please visit
VeronicaBlade.com

About Veronica Blade

Veronica Blade lives in Southern California with her husband and whichever of their kids — or someone else's kid — decides to drop in. By day she runs the family business, but each night she slips away to spin her tales. She writes stories about young adults to relive her own childhood and to live vicariously through her characters. Except her heroes and heroines lead far more interesting lives — and they are always way hotter.

You can visit Veronica Blade on Facebook and Goodreads or follow her on Twitter @VeronicaBlade. She loves hearing from readers!

For more information, visit Veronica Blade's website at www.VeronicaBlade.com.

Acknowledgements

As usual, I have so many people to be grateful for! Thank you to all my beta readers — Sara, Sausha, Juli, Kat, my niece Cassie and my mom for her fantastic suggestions. A very special thank you to author Susan Hatler for all her work on my projects and her ideas to make them even better. Susan, I love you!

Thanks to Lissa and Julie for their pre-read to make sure each of the Single Girls stories were fit to publish.

A very special thanks to Rose Nomura for her great cover design!

And my heartfelt thanks to those of you who write me to say how much you love my books. It always makes my day.

Veronica Blade